THIRTEEN FUGUES

THIRTEEN FUGUES

JENNIFER NATALYA FINK

DARK COAST PRESS
www.darkcoastpress.com
Seattle

DARK COAST PRESS

3645 Greenwood Ave N.
Seattle, WA 98103 U.S.A.
www.darkcoastpress.com | info@darkcoastpress.com

ISBN-13: 9780984428816
Library of Congress Control Number (LCCN): 2011923299
First U.S. paperback edition 2011 published by Dark Coast Press Co.

First Printing

10 9 8 7 6 5 4 3 2 1

Book design by Kate Basart, Union Pageworks

contents

for

Nadia Sohn Fink
Sarah Sohn
Nancy Ring

fugue *n. (fyüg)*

1. A *musical composition* in which one or more themes are introduced and then repeated in a complex pattern.

2. A *psychological condition* characterized by a trance state and the assumption of a new identity, sometimes accompanied by a physical or psychological journey to a previous location.

fugue

1. The dirtied bluish linens. The inherited garnet jewelry.
   The books and notes I can't possibly have written. The
   red cough syrup without a label. There is too much red
   here. I can't remember myself, can't imagine choosing
   these objects, their small histories, my preferences.

2. A musical composition in which one or more themes are
   introduced and then repeated in a complex pattern.

3. This is my bathroom, I tell the towel rack. This is not
   amnesia. I am only experiencing minor delays, like a

single-engine jet grounded due to inclement weather. Driving in aimless circles, a low-hanging fog obstructing transmission between synapses, I open and shut these cupboards, my cupboards.

4. A psychological condition characterized by a trance state and the assumption of a new identity, sometimes accompanied by a physical or psychological journey to a previous location.

5. Anything can trigger it. The scratch of a newly-trimmed mustache against my lips. A mouthful of onions, eating a pre-war breakfast in a cheap student flat in Berlin. The serious stare of a small girl; a certain shade of swimming pool blue; the glint of light on a grasshopper in early June and I speed back. But to where?

6. I brush my teeth until the gums bleed pink. In the vanity, my reflection looks vague, senseless, a word too-often repeated. I give it a confident grin. "Tanya Irene Schwartz," I declare to the mirror.

world records

Driving to the Border, Late August 1977

It's time, Tanya sings in her best T.V. theme-song voice, for world records. "The longest fingernails were grown in 1972 by Mrs. Eleanor Tayler of Lincoln, Nebraska. She is unable to wash the dishes due to her nail length, instead spending her days trimming and painting her 42-inch talons."

Tanya takes the books everywhere: the dictionary-thick *1976 Guinness Book of World Records* following her into the bathroom before they leave for Canada, *Ripley's Believe It or Not!* with the blue-skinned man leering out on the cover resting between her thighs as the car inches toward the border.

"Carl the Human Skin Bag was born with a rare deformity that causes his flesh to hang off his frame, bunching up into pockets and folds," Tanya reads loudly to Jane who sighs and looks out the window, faking disinterest.

She would skin easily. Tanya's nails mark half-moons up Jane's arms, down her thighs where they'd scratched messages to each other all summer, carving out their names in those smooth chalkboard flats just above the knee. Tanya's mouth drawing blood now, surprised by the metallic smell of it. Sororicide: sister-murder. Parricide: kinsman-killing. As they drive toward the northern border in the red Volkswagen station wagon cramped deep in the way-back, she alternates between watching the Crayolas melt into the plastic seat and tearing into Jane. Wife-killing?? Uxoricide! Uxoricide! Uxoricide! she shouts them out faster than Jane can grill her. She rolls them around against her gums like sour cherry candies, the greater the distance the root word from the -cided noun the better. Filaricide: the killing of worms.

The car tilts to the right before stopping. She always can tell when they're slowing to a stop; since her side is on the left, the seat rises up a bit as the car tilts right. She anticipates the little rise nodding against her butt as Jane's hands pinch her thighs. Those arms sheer and strong as windshield glass, eyes clamped shut for hours on the beach as nails scrape secret messages like engraved Morse code across Tanya's lightly blonded thighs. As the car veers to the right, Tanya's incisors break the surface of Jane's arm. Is human flesh kosher? she asks Rabbi Mike the next Sunday when she sits across from him in his study. Halachically, no; but in modern interpretation, it would depend whether it was take-out or prepared at home.

At home you can't mix milk with meat, eat lobster, or use lipstick made with beetle extract. Actually, you can do anything you want, as long as it's on paper plates. An overlay of paper, the whole house in a disposable smock. "Don't use the good dishes" becomes the law, the *traif* separated by the thinnest layer of white paper. Traif is garbage, food crap, pig dirt: unclean. One day their mother decides you can't store the traif in the fridge, so garbage begets garbage: a parade of traif and paper used and disposed, the good dishes resting motionless on the shelves as traif buffets dance by.

Back Home A Week Before, Ithaca, N.Y.

Play it slow. They crowd around the amplifier, Jane putting it on 33 rpm, and they wait to hear between love roller coaster and ooh ooh the supposed screams of a strangled girl oooh stretching out to five, six seconds at this speed. Outside the rec room miles of trees weigh heavy with snow, bulging like a Dr. Seuss landscape. It could be a horn, two notes, the first higher-pitched than the grace note fading it out. Or it could not really be there at all. Jane keeps moving the needle back to that last refrain, love roller coaster oooh oooh. Tanya watches deer moving between the trees outside the French windows, wondering how Jane discovered the scream. Would sororicide to find out.

Put your hand on it. Jane places Tanya's hand on the back-lit image of the wine bottle, fingers tracing the flat outline on the glossy Sunday *Times* ad. Jane sketching across the ad copy with Tanya's left index finger as she explains. The egg travels through the fallopian tubes down the slender neck of the Cabernet Sauvignon, which lies for decades in dark oak cellars, waiting for the sperm to pop them open. Jane draws the path of conception carefully across the bottle, ad copy pelted with invisible arrows and letters mapping the sojourn of first sperm, then egg. Tanya's hand dampens against the newsprint, leaving a shiny outline around the bottle. Skipping the when mommy and daddy love each other terribly much rap, Jane cuts to the chase, drawing an eyeless embryo asleep at the bottom of the wine bottle. Tanya nods as Jane sketches and explains, imagining the complicated bottle lodged in her ribs effortlessly growing eyelashes by the sixth week. The ink sticks to her fingers, blue and grey splotches of it unevenly patterning her palms and fingertips. She licks it off slowly, as though the story had permanently candied her hands.

Sex and food are the same, Jane instructs, pushing away the *Times* ad. *Anything that a man wishes to do with his wife, he may, analogously to meat that comes from the shop*, the Talmud Nedarim 20 states. It doesn't matter how you "cook" them, but rather whether or not the raw materials are themselves kosher to start with. Tanya nods her head to the rhythm of Jane's voice as she delicately licks the blue, grey, green ink off her own palms. So let's make soup. Jane separates Tanya's lips with her tongue, love roller coaster in the background ooh ooh, coasting past the unhearable scream.

Driving North of Toronto, Route 66

The world record for polygamy goes to Mr. David 'Dutch' Johnson of New Liberty, Missouri, who bragged he was the biggest bigamist. At age sixty-three when he passed away, he was married to thirty-one women at the same time—*believe it or not!"* That's trigamy times ten plus bigamy, Tanya calculates as they drive through the country darkness where trees bunch up like black grapes against the sky, miles passing between streetlights. Radio dead, speedometer deader, cigarette lighter out of juice, and Quebec is still hours away.

Tanya has won the front seat for this leg of the ride, but quickly exhausts the gadgets and stares out the V.W.'s tinted windows. The sh'mah pummeling inside Tanya's brain: *Here oh Israel the lord is god the lord is one*: everything potentially identified with everything else. Why the need for the distinction, then? she remembers him asking with that slight smirk. The lord could be *not*-god, not-one? Christianity resolves this doubt by subdividing divinity, allowing redemption through individual identification with any of the three splinters, she recalls Rabbi Mike saying, running his fingers back and forth through his thick black hair laced with oil. *Our* God, cruel god, threatens disindividuation if everything is the same, awash in oneness. But Mike, she whispers into the green-tinted night traveling past at god knows what speed, like Christianity, Judaism has its little shortcuts to heaven: forget everything but say the sh'mah each Shabbas and you're still A-OK. Jewish women need only breed and light Shabbas candles. The Messiah will ride into Jerusalem on a white horse or bull or goat when all Jewish women light shabbas candles at once. Eyelids tight against the smoke, fingers passing presto chango over the flame like a magician every Friday. Sh'mah flying through her as the quiet dark of the road blurs by.

•••

Even though it's just a local operation, the motel is fashioned to look like an American Howard Johnson's, everything imprinted with a blue and orange logo, the toilet crossed with a two-tone paper streamer announcing its official sanitization. The girls sleepily open every cabinet, pile through each brochure describing breakfast, lunch, supper, pool facilities. Bouncing on the bed, stealing the covers, they fake sleep until their parents tuck them in. Then Tanya starts. Let's Eskimo kiss, she whispers as her nose finds Jane under the yellowed sheets.

Wanting to suffer under Jane's sweet palms. To cringe as blows pelt like a low-pressure system passing across the brows. Wanting to see stars like Beetle Bailey or Dagwood, POW!, red sparklers lighting up beneath those fingers, BLAM!, invisible to her attacker. To suffer, bending around the blows and slaps, then relaxing in the rhythm of her hands. Make a fist and fit me inside it. Jane above her, suspending her between blows and kisses. Tanya bovine as a cow, placid between the uneven blows. Don't move. Don't breathe. To live on her lap. Sit still. Anchored ass to lap by her otherwise negligible weight in this pumped-up zero hour where her cheeks eagerly catch the blows hard. Porcine: pig-like. She imagines herself skinned and tanned and stretched around Jane like a shawl. Throat webby and thick around Jane's tongue, suspended in peaceful hesitation between choking and swallowing.

6 A.M., *The Next Morning*

Silently poking in the back seat. Staring straight ahead, some unwriteable rule not permitting any *mommy she's poking again*. Jane jabs Tanya in the ribs like she's drilling through to the other side. Face deadpan, serious, ignoring Tanya's wince. Tanya waits until Jane is staring out the window again. Takes the left index finger with the ragged nibbled nail and carves into the side of Jane's thigh where the flesh meets her shorts. The nail scrapes back and forth over the same spot, each time gouging in deeper.

Entering Province du Quebec! Girls, we're almost there!! Jane hums an impromptu Canada song, oh we're here in Canada yeah yeah not watching the blood trickling maps across her thigh. Tanya opens Matthew 1:3 with her other hand and reads that Jesus says eat shit and die.

He says, *nothing which entereth into a man's mouth defiles him.*

He says, *I am the resurrection.*

Anyone who believes in me even though he dies he will live.

2 A.M., Quebec

Jane is training Tanya to love total darkness. To love the way each sound magnifies in the black. To loll in Jane's voice under the covers. The first night in the fake Howard Johnson's, Jane forbids the use of the bathroom light after ten. I'm scared, Tanya whimpers.

Soon you'll hate light at night, Jane says on the second night as she unplugs the night light.

At first Tanya cries. See, says Jane, in the dark your cries are larger, more operatic. In spite of herself, Tanya listens carefully to the rhythm of her own cries. They have stanza breaks, or meter, or something; there's the hint of a pause every five or so sobs, as if she's listening for a cue, a hint as to how these tears are playing for the audience. She stops crying and suddenly must pee right now, slides off the bed onto the uncarpeted cold of the floor and feels her way towards where the bathroom was. She imagines Jesus the shit-eater leading her way, miraculously lighting her path towards the bathroom.

2 A.M., *The Next Day, At Aunt Leah's*

Tanya looks at her hands floating green-white in the chlorinated sea. Embryos must wrinkle in their briny pool, flesh puckering and peeling as cells divide and fingernails harden. "Marco!" Jane yells across the water, eyes tightly shut. "Polo!" Tanya yells back automatically. Feticide: fetus-murder. Or, more politely, aborticide. Years after a limb is lost you can feel it still, extending past the scabbed-over stub. The word for it escapes her, teasingly near her dry chlorinated tongue. So if you lost your right leg and went swimming for too long and your skin started to wrinkle up, could you feel the skin on your former right leg wrinkle, too? Her hand twitches under her gaze like a fish at the moment it notices it's no longer in water, has to think to breathe. "Marco!" Jane yells harder, her arms outstretched. Silently Tanya pulls herself out of the pool and backs into the half-open kitchen porch door, watching as Jane stumbles forward blind, waist-high in water, her Marcos echoing across the yard.

The basement covers everything in a veil of moisture. As Tanya clicks on the tape, she feels its surface dampen under her fingers. She swallows her giggles as she spreads open *Ripley's* with the bluish man on the cover between her knees. No one should know about the basement. No one has forbidden them to play down there; certainly not Aunt Leah, who spends her days smoking long cigarettes by the pool, talking past the children to their bronzing mother. They've set up an old card table down in the basement and dug up high heels and tape recorders and old board games.

❶❶

Jane gives Tanya a double nod secret signal when it's time to sneak down. But now Tanya is down there first, crouching underneath the card table, playing with her toes, waiting for Jane to discover her. She holds her breath, counting the seconds one Mississippi two Mississippi until Jane's flat feet pad down the stairs.

The tabletop is patterned with a map of North America. No one knows and no one will know: they agreed from the first trip to Aunt Leah's three, maybe four years ago about the rules of the basement. Jane is tracing around Canada with her finger, never before having ascribed a definite shape to the area above the U.S.' defining border. It's time, she sings, time for world records.

World Records

Mrs. X from Racine, Georgia failed her driver's test for the forty-seventh time, setting the known world's record for driving test failure. Let's go now to the scene of that forty-eighth try! How do you feel, Mrs. X? Tanya stop giggling or I'll slap the living shit out of you. Mrs. X?"

"Well, I'm ready, but I was ready the last forty-six times." Noise of engine, crash. Tanya scrunching tin foil to make a suitably mechanical sound. Jane's hand closing over Tanya's mouth to stop up the giggles.

"Holy mackerel! She's backed into a telephone pole! Well folks, I'm afraid Mrs. X has just broken her own previous world record, failing her driver's test for the forty-eighth time!! Do you have anything to say, Mrs. X?" Jane grips the microphone, shoving it right next to Tanya's lips but never relinquishing it.

"Well, I'll just have to practice harder and come back next week and try again!"

Tanya's feet dig into the enormous black stiletto pumps. Her hands grip the microphone away from Jane, pulling it too close to her mouth. Jane grabs the book, furiously turning the pages to their favorite Believe it or Not!

"Next, we go to Fort Tyron, Illinois, to witness the birth of the Stevenson sextuplets! We're at Fort Tyron General Hospital, watching Mrs. Stevenson give birth to six— that's right, six!—baby boys." Jane riding on top of Tanya, OK we have another boy coming out, pulling her hands out of her faded cotton underwear. Jane always the doctor. Tanya beneath her thinking of the big red car barreling out of the fake Howard Johnson's, the road scrambling past. Tanya always all six sextuplets. In the mossy dark, sounds magnify. Without light, the basement looms out borderless, yet she senses the layers of piled-up junk hovering oppressively close. Fist probing in, oh I feel a head, two heads, now push! Breathe! Push! Jane's pink polished nails scraping in, carving out messages to the unborn. Emergency procedure! The baby's stuck! We'll have to use the scalpel now. Tanya feels Jane's fist unfolding, each finger a separate organism.

"Oh my god! One has two heads! It's stuck up your ass now! I can't get it out! Doctor!" Jane is sweating and barking and the tape is still running. Tanya squeezes her eyes shut. She can feel herself rising up now, can see the double-headed baby popping out, projected like a film on the split-screen of her own white ass. Twisting anxiously around to catch the images curving over the cheeks. In full color, fading like denim, as old film will. Jane and Tanya. And then it slides away, back into the crack.

Suicide: self-murder. Jane gets up suddenly, face looming wet and red. Runs up the stairs. Sin of sins. Tanya hears the splash of Jane bellyflopping off the diving board. For Christians, the sin lies not in harming God's great creation but in the necessary doubt, in failing to believe in redemption. *Ripley's* lies under Tanya's bare ass now, pages creased past rescue. Doubt, free will, suicide: an unholy trinity snaking around Augustinian Christian belief. John Donne suggests that Jesus was a suicide, she recalls Rabbi Mike saying with the smirk that always accompanies any mention of Jesus. Think of it: *My God, My God, Why have you forsaken me?* In Judaism, suicide is *verboden*, considered a violation of one's contract with the community. However, there is no explicit prohibition against suicide in our Bible. In fact, the Biblical passage upon which the traditional Talmudic prohibition is based says only *And surely your blood of your lives will I require; at the hand of every beast will I require it; and at the hand of every man, even at the hand of every man's brother, will I require the life of man.*

God wants your hands and blood. God wants your life. The sweat on Jane's body floats on the surface of the pool, each drop containing all of Jane's genetic code. The rewinding whir of the tape recorder grinds into Tanya's ears as she pulls up her bathing suit. Jane swims underwater laps, her sweat swimming above her. And the world record for multiple births goes to Mrs. Y of Fort Tyron, Illinois.

Ten Years Later, 30,000 Feet Over the Atlantic

On the El Al flight to Tel Aviv the religious gather on the left side of the plane to face Jerusalem as they pray, crowding the aisles as the stewardesses purse their lips and barrel through with plastic containers of orange juice. Tanya feels a little lurch leftwards as she swallows down the acidic juice in one gulp. She imagines Jane in her small bungalow in North Tel Aviv, surrounded by her three children. Tracing ads for Israeli brands of wine to demonstrate conception. Each child having a turn at it, the glossy newsprint sweating into their small fingers. No, that's the wrong picture. Jane's in the hospital now, slowly recovering from miscarrying child number four. Noah saved God.

The plane lurches forward. Northerly, according to the map projected against the wall showing a little plane icon inching its way toward Tel Aviv. Saved God, excitable God, our poor Lord stalked by that awful grinding sense of exhaustion and failure that follows the completion of any big project. Jane plumper now, rarely showing her thighs beneath her hausfrau dresses and corporate suits. Jane in charge: barking in Hebrew to her daughters, her husband, her god each shabbas. The stewardesses are shepherding the clump of praying men back to their seats, promising kosher chicken wings within minutes.

Is human flesh kosher? *God regretted having made man on earth.* Is suddenly hypersensitive to his Creation's little faults. So Noah made the ark, loaded up his two-by-two zoo, to show God that Creation wasn't so bad. But God has his price. *I give you everything*, he says with a slight smile, *with this exception: you must not eat flesh with life, that is to say blood, in it.* And God promises to never, ever, have such a terrible tantrum again. Tanya pulls down her tray, graciously accepting her kosher chicken wings with hot sauce. But you know how those promises go. Made in that velvet hour after forgiveness, all kisses and contrition. The plane lurches sideways a bit, even though the religious are all seated now, munching loudly. She reels off the lists, trying to still her mind. Deicide: God-murder. Regicide: king-murder. Vatricide: prophet-killing. Mariticide: spouse-murder, especially of a husband. Love roller coaster, oooh ooh. No English word for the special killing that makes it kosher. Can't remember the Hebrew. Couldn't ask Jane, her mouth and hands unavailable, wrapped in the hospital melodrama of miscarriage. Unaskable.

Tanya thinks of turning to the Orthodox man next to her with his trim beard and black hat who is now carefully wiping the hot sauce off his lips, imagines asking him for that word. But she might get other words, interrogating her clearly shaky relationship to observance, so she remains silent. If only Jane's thighs were here. Jane's blonde thighs straddling Tanya's, weighing her down as her hands pull Tanya's hair. The weight of the thighs counter-balancing the pulling up of the fingers. Perfectly balanced. The plane icon inches toward Tel Aviv. Jane's sweet thighs upon her, that elegant stillness which comes with fear, that slow cutting off of circulation. And then Tanya's thighs: stinging, white and bloodless from the pinching, while her hair is pulled to the point of follicle damage. The world record for kosher pinching goes to Miss T of New York.

healy

The thick, clay-like kind that came in white jars with a red brush stuck inside the top was the easiest to procure and the most similar to real food, all sweet and gritty on the tongue like an undercooked vanilla cake. But Elmer's in orange-tipped bottles, sipped straight down or half-dried, licked off my coated fingers; Elmer's watery white in clear plastic bottles, leaving an aftertaste of chemicals that made me wild for more all day: Elmer's was not an experiment but a passion. In first grade, learning to wait my turn, to line up with the others, to pronounce 's' and 'sh' distinctly, glue became my goal. Who knows

●●

when I first tasted its sweet unmilky flow, but when I did, I knew I needed it more than the four food groups we'd draw in bright pastels. Gobs of it, surprisingly unsticky when mixing with my mouth's fresh saliva, glue glorious glue, my secret goal.

Glue organized my school day. From tracing the already well-known alphabet to collaging the Niña, Pinta, and Santa Maria, every drab of knowledge might be an opportunity to sequester a sip or slug of it.

"Are you hungry? Do they feed you enough in the morning?" Mrs. Healy and her ever-changing eyeshadowed lids ask one day, taking me aside, showing me the secret drawer in her desk where she keeps her lunch, to which I am now welcome if I am hungry.

I don't cry. I concentrate on not crying, my cheeks hot pink, shame repeating like a song in my ears. Caught. I am silent, eyes staring back at her green-shadowed lids, my hazel eyes filling with water, answerless. She frees me, and I go to lunch with the others, but my lust is doubly secret now, thrilled up with the new possibility of being caught glue-handed. Not of the consequences of being caught, but of the being caught, of the kindness of interrogation.

To paraphrase Freud: where glue was, interrogation goes. After my private tour of Mrs. Healy's lunch (an apple, a vanilla yogurt, and carrot and celery sticks in separate plastic bags) I grow extravagantly careless. I leave the drained-out bottles in plain sight on top of my desk, collecting the red brushes stuck to the tops for two weeks, then using them as the eyes of space monsters in our class collage of Apollo X. When she's eyeing me again during social studies, pencil eyebrows lifting up over the pearlescent lids, I become all smiley smart kid, arm shooting up, aching to tell the class the difference between horizontal and vertical. Inside the desk I finger the prize: four brand new extra large Elmer's, taken in plain view during art class. Fingering my booty in the back of the coat closet at home, I imagine Mrs. Healy taping me up, sealing my fingers and mouth together with some super superglue. And she did.

Yes, yes, Mrs. Healy.

Yes, yes, Mrs. Healy, I repeat after her, the "s's" sticking to my tongue. I still crave that game, crave the final "s" that grips tongue to mouth until you're so sticky with it she has to let you go.

I started speaking early, quickly, and in paragraphs. Nonetheless, the lisp saturated my speech so thoroughly that only my sister Jane could understand me. Jane became my official translator. I spoke and their eyes would turn to her. Little girls grow out of these things, my parents reasoned. Little girls lose extra syllables like baby fat.

In first grade at Northern Elementary School I went to see Mrs. Healy after recess at 1:30 on alternate Wednesdays in the white and green trailer house attached to the main beige brick building. It was just that sort of '70s rural school: cows in the front yard fenced off from the playground, trailer house attached in back for Special Ed. I remember nothing of how I unlearned my lisp there. I do know for certain that on each alternate Wednesday, Mrs.

Healy wore a different sparkly shade of blue or pink or green eyeshadow all the way up to her thin arched brows.

And the stick. She never threatened or hit with it; she simply pointed it at the hard "s" words on the pages of my reader. Her stick was too thick and long to be easily manipulated, so it would jostle around in her hands as she'd point, its orange-varnished surface glinting with the light from the fluorescents overhead.

Yes, yes, Mrs. Healy.

Yes, yes, Mrs. Healy. Jane started the game, and "Yes, yes, Mrs. Healy" immediately became its official name. All of Jane's games had official names. It was the summer I was obsessed with finding hidden dumbwaiters in restaurants and stripping down to my underwear in the cold empty auditoriums in the seaside science community where Dad had taken us so he could do his research. Jane was always Mrs. Healy. The other researchers' kids were younger than her and boys and liked the idea of messing up Daddy's forbidden lecture hall. We were all Miss and Mister to her when Jane stood up there, hair pulled into a tight bun, perspiring around her thin lips. With the long pointer she'd stand at the lectern and assign us our tasks. Whatever she said, you had to respond, "Yes, yes, Mrs. Healy."

I was the projectionist. My job was to follow Mrs. Healy's motions with the slide projector, keeping the hot oval just below her neck so that she wouldn't be blinded. She would yell, "Lights!" and I would twirl the projector onto her thin lips as I responded with "Yes, yes, Mrs. Healy," carefully shaping each "s" with my tongue and teeth. She glowed in that oval, the metal braces on her front teeth spraying the light back over us all as we waited for our next instructions. I'd hide in the corner of the lecture hall behind the rows of blue fold-out chairs with my slide projector, excitedly pulling off my clothes, waiting for certain failure and its stick.

I liked my job pretty well, especially the part where I'd get tired and forget to say "Yes, yes, Mrs. Healy" and be called up by her to take the stick. I'd close my eyes as the orange wood tickled the back of my throat where my tonsils had been, thinking of the blues and pinks and greens of Mrs. Healy's eyelids as she pointed out the final "s's". It never splintered but sometimes Jane would have to have a string of kids in a row take it: "Mr. Andrew! Mr. Scott! Miss Tanya! None of you are addressing me correctly! Have you forgotten the rules?" and we would line right up, swallowing each other's saliva with the wood, not daring to spit it out in her presence.

Yes, yes, Mrs. Healy.

"Say it." Her rage was smooth, quick, absolute. The beads of sweat would gather on her part, a shallow river dividing the two halves of her brown-haired skull as she'd bend over us and the piss would squirt out of my thin grey underpants. Drying off in my corner under the oval projection light I would murmur "Yes, yes, Mrs. Healy" to myself, wanting it to never end, wanting to stand beneath her forever with the saliva of the other kids dripping slowly against my throat where the "s's" now emerge clearly when bidden at the end of each word.

vertebrae

i. Bad Plumbing

Tanya's walls spurt piss. The yellow bleeds daily from the walls' recently painted pores. Between dinner and bedtime, while Tanya is in the kitchen or playing out in the yard, the walls piss all over the room.

A plumbing problem, something to do with the basement pipes backing up, their father assures them as they swallow down breakfast. It's a Sunday, so he is in Mr. Fixit

●●

mode, eager to devise the perfect experiment to track the wall piss to its origin. Blue dye #3. The solution, he announces over bagels and lox with a smile, is blue dye #3. This house has always had crappy plumbing, he says with authority. But we're gonna fix all that with the help of our trusty blue dye #3. By noon the two bathrooms are rigged with blue food coloring, every flush turning the bowl into a tropical ocean floor.

•••

Tanya's walls spurt blue piss. Her white furniture spattered in it, walls unevenly coated from ceiling to floor with spirals and drips. Something angry is written in the script-like twists of the spatter, its patterns too thorough to be random. Unmechanical.

Her perfect white dresser took the brunt of it, as though a pipe full of blue dye #3 had opened its veins directly onto its thickly painted top. Tanya figures that adding another color to the mess won't matter, so she polishes the white knobs of the dresser's six drawers with Maybelline Frosted Peach. The chemical-coated perfumes of the nail polish mix with the piss smell. Tanya puts on a second layer, the frosted peach knobs turning a deep orange, noticing as she leans close to the dresser to prevent drips that the blue is shot through with green. It's okay; green is my favorite color, she practices saying to them as she inhales.

ii. Bad Back

"Kiss me."

"Just one kiss. Or a hug. Just one."

I'll tell. Tanya shrinks away from the imploring eyes, the sugary voice stained with an acid aftertaste. She backs into the orange counter that divides the eat-in kitchen, her lips not quite forming the two words. I'll tell.

"Well then you can at least walk on my back. It's so sore, you can't imagine, every muscle is mixed up with the bones like some hideous malformed rock. Pleeeze? Come on—the Doctor says it's good for the scoliosis."

Breccia. Tanya removes her sneakers but not her socks. Jane collapses on the floor face down, arms outstretched, ass waving fat and high. Breccia rocks contain both igneous and other unrelated rock formations. Tanya imagines the nerves twisting between the vertebrae, gripping each piece of bone. Jane's back is splayed beneath her, stiff as a balance beam, but snaky. Tanya practices her gold medal routines on it, stretching her arms and pointing her toes with a graceful Nadia Comenici smile for her fans. Her toes wobble in the space between the vertebrae. She tries to detect the twist of scoliosis under her feet, the exotic islands of bone clumped together amidst the muscle tissue, deviating from a straight line.

"Kiss me."

Begging even as Tanya's heels dig in between the uneven segments of spine. Begging until she's hoarse. Tanya unanswering, her soles feeling the little pimples and rough dry patches sprinkled across Jane's back as she does exaggerated arabesques, smiling with all her big teeth toward the invisible Olympic judge's box. I'll tell.

"Ow!" Jane is shaking with pain, back crumpling beneath Tanya's gyrations. Tanya mouths it as she continues her routine, not looking to see if Jane can even see her. Her feet pounding it into her with every turn. Not needing to say it out loud. I'll tell.

iii. Bad Foundations

The two girls stand outside the house beside their mother in identical coats printed with fake Incan rug patterns, topped by matching fuzzy angora berets knitted by Aunt Susan. Jane's coat and hat are pink, Tanya's as always are green. Mom's hat is beige, almost the same wheat shade as her tightly curled hair and her well-worn rabbit coat from which she pulls loose hairs as she rambles on. "OK girls, let's be calm. The house is contaminated but we're safe out here." The girls are silent, letting her pretend that it is they who need consolation. "We'll wait here until Dad comes home. Everything will be fine in no time." Tanya rubs her soft green head, fingers remembering the glamorous satin feel of Susan's long hair.

They are outside the house, watching it for signs of flood or fire. Only minutes ago Tanya and her mother were driving home from Tanya's ballet class. Only seconds ago they were pulling into the garage in the red Volkswagen station wagon with its peeling "Pollution Stinks" bumper sticker, Mom ready to prepare dinner, Tanya anticipating a clean shower in her remodeled bathroom. Only nanoseconds between entering the living room, smelling it, and pulling Jane from her bedroom out into the driveway. The blue has spread to the living room, Tanya announces. It could carry germs, e-coli, bacteria. It could be flammable. Tanya watches her mother and sister watch the house, imagining how a photo of this moment would look, all three lined up with matching hats and eyes all staring straight into the house.

Their mother stands erect in the remains of the bunny coat, looking more cow than rabbit now that the fur is patching off, leaving stretches of tanned skin colored the same brown as her big eyes. Tanya snuggles closer, rubbing her cheek against a big patch of furless leather. The house has all the lights on, abandoned in the middle of its evening with the dishwasher still running. Another family might be inside now, just out of sight, making use of the light shooting through the house's sockets, exhaling carbon monoxide, shedding skin and hair in microscopic quantities with each passing second. Perhaps the house needs such minute human waste to function, Tanya thinks.

The juiced-up bright green Volkswagen Beetle drives up. "Why are you guys outside?" he asks. The blue has spread, their mother explains. Oh Daddy, I'm scared the house is sick, Jane says as she grasps his hand. Tanya walks with him to the door, protesting when he doesn't let her come inside with him to investigate. You girls wait in the car. We'll clean up this mess and go get a pizza.

It's that damn foundation, he tells them over the mushroom and eggplant pizza. It's shifted again and screwed up the plumbing. The foundation can't support the weight of the house. I don't even want to bother to fix it; it'd be like operating on a sore knee when you have a spinal cord injury.

The house's back is broken, Tanya tells herself that night.

iv. Bad Target

Seated on the floor reading Dickens, Tanya feels her enter, not raising her eyes from Little Nell. She likes to read on the floor, no distracting fabric to root her to the outside world. She practices keeping her back perfectly straight while she reads, lining up the vertebrae like neat stacks of undershirts, folded and ready to be put away. Stack, stack, she uncrunches as she reads. She is being watched and targeted again. She looks up and sees the hands raised, the clear glass pitcher of blue piss-water clutched behind the head, the knees slightly bent. Ready, aim, fire. Their eyes meet. Tanya returns to the book, extends her neck and lets the house swim away as the blue spatters against the wall. Tanya doesn't watch as Jane heads for the bathroom to wait for the blue to finish flowing.

The knobs of the dresser are spattered with it, but the bed with its green-and-white checked cover took the brunt this time. Gallons of blue piss saturate the bed straight through to the mattress, leaving it spongy to the touch. Tanya pokes the bed in the center, watching a small pool of blue liquid accumulate around the concave depression.

camp

Fortress

The foundation's crap. Goyishe shit foundation, Dad decrees each spring in earshot of Grandpa, swearing shirtless and cross-armed as he cleans out the basement and rigs up three different alarm systems.

They opened Twin Willows in Queens in 1960, exactly six years to the day before I was born, on the day after Memorial Day. And oy, did we ever labor with you! my

●●

grandmother would inevitably joke, confusing Memorial with Labor Day. From the start, it was a commie kid camp, for post-red diaper babies whose parents couldn't afford something more Connecticut. To compensate, they named it Twin Willows, even though only untwinned maples and evergreens surrounded the camp, which was surrounded by barbed wire fences.

I always just called it "camp." I loved camp. My sister Jane preferred to spend her summers in expensive ballet camps, pirouetting and leaping for eight hours a day, but I remained faithful to Grandma and Grandpa's Twin Willows Camp for New Youth. Camp consisted of an arts and crafts hut, an animal hut, a modern dance hut, a pool, and no sports. Proud of no sports. The whole complex was electronically wired directly to the police station, a novelty in Queens. A small fortune sunk into wirings. A small fortress built on a loan from the East New York Immigrant's Savings Bank that would only be paid off after their death.

Crib

I sleep in the crib even though I am ten. There is no other bed for me at camp, and it has become a habit. Besides, I am too grown-up to complain. It is a small crib, made smaller each year by the books I pile in with me every night. I would curl against the wooden bars, playing monkey-in-the-zoo by day, feeling my limbs stick together at night, wondering if I'd awaken to find my legs welded together into an abstract sculpture. The Nazis will come for you, says my father with cocky certainty, so don't hide it. The Nazis came for you, says Grandma as she vacuums, shrieking a bit because her hearing aid is turned way up, so you may as well admit it.

Jewish, Jew, Jewess. I try out each one, rolling the J's under my tongue. In the crib I dream of a mustachioed S.S. officer wearing shiny gold cuff links that clink against the bars. I am chained to the bars, unable to escape as his mustache grazes my mouth my thighs and whoosh I'm left sweaty and disappointed as I awaken to the swoosh whoosh sounds of my grandfather cleaning out the hamster cages in the animal hut below my bedroom window.

Grandpa's uncooked whole onions and gefilte fish stink through the house each morning at breakfast. Grandma's overcooked filet mignon with onions burns the air for dinner. The little white crib is my haven, lightly scented with decades-old baby powder. Lying in a fetal scrunch so as not to bang the sides of the crib, I inhale the white powdery aroma and feel the bars the alarms the barbed wire tucking me in, safe and sound.

Breaking, Entering

The thieves entered anyway, four times, crawling straight into Grandma and Grandpa's third-floor bedroom. The burglars must have predicted the lag-time between their entry and the arrival of the cops, I think as I study the broken yellow and red wires the morning after the first break-in. Experts themselves at wiring, they managed to silence the alarms in the house.

Each time Grandma and Grandpa slept through it, undisturbed until the cops shook them awake. Each night they slept with public radio blaring, strands of crisply accented BBC news mixing with their snores, audible across the hall in my crib long after three A.M. The thieves took the ruby earrings out of Grandma's legally deaf ears one at a time, slowly unhooking her heavy rubies so as not to disturb her eardrum. Their hands on one lobe, then the other, working fast to the clipped British beat of news flashing from Vietnam or Dusseldorf. Never caught in the act, the goods never recovered. It's just as well, Dad assures them; who knows what those barbarians might have done if you had awakened. Gold filigreed hoops were quickly inserted where the rubies had been.

My father remained the primary invader of that fortress, able to enter it at will without setting off alarms. "He courted this damn house for years," my Aunt Louise cackled, telling me again the story of how, in high school, my father figured out how to break in without setting off the alarms. I thought of this as I watched him fix the broken wires after the first burglary. He'd broken its secret codes long before the thieves came. He knew its secrets, knew which windows triggered only my mother in her tight sweater and Marilyn curls. And he still relished his prowess. Out late at the lab, even though he had the front door key now, he'd climb up the fire-escape and slip in without disturbing so much as a single wire. I was still a novice.

No one ever saw him enter, but he'd brag about it the next morning at breakfast. "*Any* fool can break into this dump," he'd bark proudly as my grandmother poured his coffee. "Well if you're so smart, Einstein, how come you can't build us a better mousetrap then, eh? Some hotshot scientist you are—can't even build a damn alarm," my grandfather snorts while my grandmother turns down her hearing aid.

After each break-in I would sneak into the basement after breakfast and rearrange the boxes of straws, building pyramids and fortresses, pretending I'm Anne Frank waiting to be tortured, then arranging the straws into bundles tied with hair ribbons of five, ten, twenty-three, each number symbolizing a different voodoo curse on my father. No one ever commented on the pink and orange hair ribbons left tied around the straws.

Festival Days

Iiii don't want a pickle, just wanna ride on my motorsickle. Iii don't want to die, just want to ride on my motorcy—cle. Head Counselor Elaine loves that song. Elaine's father runs a kosher pickle farm in south Jersey, so we each get a whole full sour to sing with on Arlo and Woody Guthrie Appreciation Festival.

The Festival Days, held every Friday, complete with parades and pickles, were our yacht club and our Shabbas. Every Friday we'd dance and sing and parade across Twin Willows, performing Grandma's belief in the superiority of gefilte fish and social justice to *shul* and tennis whites. Parades against South African apartheid where we call and respond. Parades with white candles and my mother dancing in a sheer orange leotard to commemorate the Six Million. After the parades, snack time: one red or blue popsicle doled out by Grandma herself, each getting his due, no child getting more or less than his fair share of her popsicles. "Each gets only his due, Tanya," my grandmother repeats as I stand in line for a second time. Nestled on top of Elaine's thighs, I suck in the red goo, then run off to piss in the house. I asked for no other special privileges, but I could only piss in the basement bathroom of the house with the boxes of Sweetheart straws lined up behind me. I'd rush through the arts and crafts hut, through the animal hut, ignoring the baby gerbils as I hurried toward that piss.

Pool

A special animal hut housed the gerbils. Sometimes bunnies, mice, spiders, or hamsters, too, but only the gerbils could be counted on to survive the August heat and constant rough kid-handling. Every morning Grandpa got up at 4:30 to feed the gerbils and clean the pool. Awakened by his gargling in the bathroom, I'd follow him outside, leaning against the fence.

They stare at us through the barbed wire: them, outside, loud and sweaty, full of Jake's Package Store sour balls, and us, inside camp, skinny Schwartzs and Kleins and Feldsteins mixed with mixed-marriage middle-class Afro-Americans imported in from the City to color up us pale commiekids. *Honky candy-ass jew kike slut we'll rape your white shit face.* We would spy them over the wire fence as we pushed each other off the high dive, but we never spoke to them or responded to their threats and curses. Only in the early morning, when there'd be seven or eight of them and one of me, would they do more than just stare in to the camp. *Jew faggot cocksucker pussy-faced whore.*

Every spring my father painted the pool the same light blue, shirtless as he rolled the thick paint all the way down to the twelve foot mark. Draining it and painting it, he conquered its crumbling cement with his paint and brushes each spring. He would reek with the mixture of kid piss and chlorine for the rest of the summer. His usual scientist smell still discernible, but turned, like a new car's interior gone sour, only returning to its fresh chemical scent when we returned to Ithaca in the fall.

Disaster contaminated his pool, that second-to-last summer at camp. My eyes open to the red flash of alarms reflecting off the walls. Mom drapes her own bathrobe over me, drags me out of the crib, out to camp. Dad is in the pool, swimming through a gerbil sea. We watch them in silence, their furry bodies lumping up to the surface like an oil spill. He rises up, face scratched in the rescue mission. Of the thirty gerbils dumped into the pool by the neighborhood kids, only three are saved. They stole nothing, Grandma repeats to the police over the phone. Not even a single gerbil is missing; all are accounted for, either stone dead or shrieking road-kill screams as Dad dries them off with a beach towel. We stand in the kitchen, Mom discarding the dead gerbils, Dad dripping onto the linoleum floor as Grandma orders the police to come catch the criminals. Grandpa sleeps through it all, dreaming to the calm voice of the BBC's early edition.

"Did you save the bunny?" Grandma asks. "She's pregnant, and the kids are waiting for the babies." Dad, still fully clothed, wetter than the gerbils, dutifully dives back in, fishing her out from the bottom of the pool. Exhausted, he plops her dead wet body on the good oak kitchen table, where we aren't even allowed to eat popsicles. The rabbit's fur is matted tight to her skin. I can make out little bulges where the babies are. Can fetuses drown? How can something never born experience death? I don't ask these questions. I wish the dead pregnant bunny could come sleep with me in my crib, dry its fur off against my pillow.

Amidst the chaos I duck into the basement bathroom, grabbing a handful of Sweetheart straws to line the crib. I place their wrappings at the corners of my mattress, their thin paper wisping out like the shards of an empty wasp's nest. If I were drowning, I would have to conserve oxygen. I stick five straws in my mouth and try to breathe as little as possible, letting the air trickle out of my nose in microscopic increments. Nestled against the wrappers, straws dangling between my lips, I fall asleep.

Grandpa gets up at 4:30 the next morning and makes his usual rounds, first refilling the container of straws in the bathroom, then phoning all over the city, frantically trying to find fresh gerbils in late August. My father spends the morning draining the pool while my grandmother vacuums up the cop's muddy tracks on the carpet. My mother sleeps until noon. I sit in the kitchen waiting for lunch, making a braid out of three straws. I don't know what became of the rabbit.

Next year we'll try guard dogs, Grandma yells above the vacuum. Next year in Jerusalem, my father shoots back from the pool. Next year.

bikini

The sun is burning red welts into the skin left uncovered by my green bikini. My tampon, some cheap Brazilian brand that smells like burnt hair, is slipping out, stiffly pressing its way out of my lycra green-covered crotch as I lie on my peeling back. She wore an itsy-bitsy teeny-weenie, I sing as I burn. What would surely have shamed me in Ithaca, NY, I thoroughly relished in São Paolo, Brazil: mock erections, mock sunstrokes, mock suicides, authentic sadisms, smelly cunts . . . I hate writing about my adolescence. Except for Brazil. Except for the

●●

almost-pure hatred I fashioned in my green bikini in my red body that summer before I was thirteen.

Each day I fight with them, scream Portuguese obscenities in public, threaten murder or suicide or both, always disappearing into foreign crowds at dangerous moments, moments when Cousin Mauricio the Communist says the fascists run the neighborhood samba demonstration by which we're suddenly surrounded, instants in the *favelas* where seven-year-old whores crowd around my father's tightly jeaned crotch, seconds where my sister is plucking her eyebrows completely out in the bathroom of the National Forest Park with its oversized tropical flora and fauna fuck it yes I disappear screaming just fuck you. I scream as I race through the park with its heavy palms, hiding in the john for hours screaming in hot sputters over what?

There are no pictures of me from this trip. I threatened to break the camera of he who dared to picture me (well, just one, standing on the beach with my pubic hair peeking out of my tight green bikini bottom, mouth opening in snarling resistance to the flash bulb, tampon visibly pressing up in sarcastic erection, palm trees unevenly framing me so that they appear to be closing in, circling the triangle of green cloth with its lacy necklace of stray hairs).

slipping

Can women rape men? The smell of bacon sizzling fills the air of the campus student union where the Ithaca Association of Jewish Studies holds its earnest Sunday afternoon youth education seminars. Tanya refuses to call it Sunday school; despite the bacon and the hippie teachers, she insists on *shul*, demands to be placed in the class with the older kids because the guy who does real Talmud and modern Hebrew who cracks jokes about reform Jews with their organ players and ecumenical English prayers, Judaism lite, Christianity without Christ, Mike-someone with thick black sideburns, not a rabbi but a true rebbe teacher, Ph.D. in maybe Yiddish, Mike does older kids only.

This week, we'll talk about women's liberation, Rashi, and Isaiah 3:13. I think, he says with a smile not quite at her, that what Rashi really means here is, can women rape men?

1979-Upstate New York-Training for the Bat Mitzvah

Can women rape men? In the morning before shul in the room her mother decorated in yellow checkers Tanya's fingers repeat the wet question angering the furry sides picturing the section of the Talmud black bold-faced questions blunt across the page: If your neighbor is re-tiling his roof and it is hot so he gets naked then slips perhaps his feet are sweaty because of the heat and below him she is lying on her back on a yellow-checked picnic blanket also naked because of the heat and he slips his sweaty body falling over hers her hand rubbing fast reddening her face boiling up under the yellow and white comforter who yes who is liable if he falls onto her penetrates her quite by accident their sweat mingling only for a minute but the damage is done unintentional but because of the heat he slipped she's raped damaged who is liable her hand grabbing for the answer as she comes it flashes in black and white like a newspaper headline: Can women rape men?

All night Mike dreams of fucking his brother Josh. Coming on his sweet undead face, some form of frontal intercourse that does not involve penetration really it's like fucking Malka all the familiar positions just with Josh's smile, Josh's short thick body where Malka would be squeezing out against the sheets but Mike just awakens hard and confused running to piss in the bathroom that smells like her deodorant. The first fuck Josh dream since his death.

Basically, you talk. It begins with a series of questions. "So what does this week's portion tell us?" Before your coat is off, before he leads you to the little windowless study between the bedroom with the ancient lace coverlet and the metallic bathroom, before you dissect the portion or learn some bit of ritual or history or Hebrew, you talk. And answer.

Even in the subzero chill factor upstate winters with their endless student suicides, Mike Silverstein always seemed to be sweating. Sweating and talking: the words pushing moisture through his black hair, soaking his kipah, his mustache. Tanya has never seen a mustache as black and thick as his. They start at four on Sundays and Wednesdays and talk Torah until one of her parents remembers to pick her up at seven or eight. They hate all the driving but figure two shots of hippie Jewdom a week will inoculate her against Christmas trees and local boys with bad teeth and snowmobiles. The only drop of Torah, Mishnah, and Gmorah she will remember is one minor portion regarding Jewish law's stance on the ethical and legal repercussions of putting glass on your fence.

To keep your sheep in. And your neighbor is injured. Also that there are fifteen different interpretations from the mystical to the legal and back and can women rape men?

In today's portion there are seven commentaries on liability in sexual matters. There is sweat dripping beneath his scalp, threading along his black hair and mustache. Even though injured virgins and glass on fences may not seem relevant, each commentary tries to interpret it in relation to larger social issues. He is looking past her serious nodding head toward the window above her chair. Josh's chest sweaty against his. The room soundless. Their chests glued together, everything heavy and wet. He cannot remember a single mole on that chest, though he suspects there were many. Only the sweat, the sweat stinking into the sheets the next morning every morning he knows every note of its scent.

Can women rape men? he asks as they talk past the time when her mother's battered red Volkswagen with its peeling *Pollution Stinks* sticker should whisk her out of his driveway past Talmudic debate towards a fresh salad served up on the good oak table in the orange shag living room. Daylight has passed and the study is dark and perhaps if there were like ten women and one guy or a girl with a gun and one guy she can't see his even features or his thick black mustache and the mechanics are fuzzy: a group of tall blonde women driving up leaping out tackling him down knocking his kipah off dozens of long red nails ripping his black hair from the scalp as they pull down his pants then the mechanics fuzz up the frame. But you can't *make* him hard, he says under his breath and yeah she nods like she knows this the disappointment washing through her.

She suddenly feels the want the fierce want for women to be able to rape men. On principle. I mean, you can't force him to shoot, he says louder. She misses the way he's watching her, doesn't catch the way his mouth is hanging in waiting remembering Josh's eyes squinting closed as he is fucked solid. He has a habit she has noticed of stroking the hairs on his left forearm with his right hand when he concentrates. No, she talks as he strokes it, no I guess not quite rape then, but they could take him by force up his asshole or something, right?

A man is shingling a roof and it is hot so he gets naked. On the grass beneath him, a woman is also getting hot and gets naked and he slips and falls on her and she is slippery from the Hawaiian Tropic Extra Dark coconut tanning oil and he slips right in and she wants damages. Can she collect?

What if she were on the roof sweaty and shingled and he were oiled up and waiting below? The Talmud is quite specific on this, he tells her as the red Volkswagen drives up. Read it for next time and tell me how you think this applies today. I'll give you a hint, he winks as she walks toward the car: it has something to do with the fundamental difference between Christianity and Judaism.

It is a peeing contest that doesn't end. Poised as far from the bowl as they could get, rated on arc as well as distance. Josh is the messy one, splattering on the white tile, aim off from his inevitable giggling. Malka turns toward him in her sleep, curled around herself. They sneak the usual glances down, yes, but it's actually their pee arching over, intersecting above the bowl, that fascinates Mike. An elaborate Olympic-style ratings system is developed that he tries to recall during the funeral but it is the details of the arc that he remembers instead: Mike's perfect curve intersecting Josh's wiggling line. Inside Malka her body all wet and muscle he rocks back there, watching the funeral watching what is no longer Josh disappear.

She is watching Charlie's Angels jiggle toward the camera, asking herself the question she will ask all future lovers: which Angel do you like the best? There is Farrah who everyone likes, fair like the blind scales of justice they teach you in social studies. She smiles back at Farrah as she reaches for the chips. Or Kelly, almost boyish, almost bright. She never chooses Kelly. Then there's Sabrina, also the name of Sabrina the Teenage Witch on Saturday morning cartoons. Like the witch, Sabrina is the brunette. Sabrina's red lipstick and arched eyebrows smirk into the camera, hinting at something too rank for prime time. A husky bit of air whistles between her perfect teeth before each predictable line. Oh, Charlie! Really! I'd never! Charlie's Angels never see Charlie, who directs them to knock out the bad guys while knocking back a frosty drink between the bosoms of two bikinis. The difference between Judaism and Christianity, it turns out, is that for Christians sin is a kind of, well, existential state his hand waves to underscore *state* his lips curling a bit as she sits across him beneath the window watching watching whereas it is one's conscious *will*, one's choices and intentions, not the mere fact of being human that are sinful in Judaism.

A man tiling a roof slips and falls into a quick rape but did not intend it, did not even think of it, so while he is economically liable for damages he is not *morally* liable; he has broken something rather than sinned against it, ruled Rabbi Akiba in 1438. Asleep but for a hand cupping his balls, softly first then too hard. Malka likes to wake Mike before the alarm already perfumed and lipsticked. Perfectly put together, he always thinks as he rolls onto her, still asleep but for the hand. And hours later he shifts in his chair remembering the hand too hard watching this child pull her long mousy hairs into her mouth sucking their ends desperate to understand two types of liability. Always a little desperate to learn. Sabrina could be a Jew. With those intentional eyebrows, that sucking noise aiming to undercut Farrah's jiggles. Definite Jew.

Manchester, England, 1979

She is not permitted to hear him. See him, yes: talking and moving inside the grainy screen like any other paunchy earnest public figure. But where at home *fuck* and *shit* would be dubbed out, his whole voice not his words or his "free speech" but his voice cannot ever be heard. His mouth chews up words fast but by British Broadcasting Regulation a voice with a mild Irish lilt is dubbed in unsynchronized with his quick mouth she watches it moving and stopping before and after the stranger's voice. In the beginning there was darkness. Hear oh Israel the Lord is God the Lord is One. His voice is two. The state-supplied voice heard and the unhearable One. She watches him after school each day on the news, wondering how they chose this rather calming voice: did they audition hundreds of Northern Irish middle-aged Catholic actors, roomfuls of Gerry Adams look-alikes practicing militant Republican speeches in the corners of the T.V. station's office, waiting their turn patiently as Gerry never would. Does this voice "actually" approximate Gerry's or is it precisely a certain quantity of difference from Gerry's that they're after? Or is it this dissolving, this sliding away from content that this dubbing produces, which the censors demand? His voice, not his words censored.

God's voice is unhearable. Unbearable. God demanded Abraham sacrifice his son, not like the other gods in town who need blood to make new men, who need blood to produce their much-vaunted love, no our God cruel God doesn't *need* this sacrifice. There is no reason for it. Except for the senseless, unreasonable desire to see Abraham's willingness to kill his son for no reason. Nowadays, the Book dubs God, appears in his place, where His voice would be. God is silent now. At school they get new notebooks with greenish pages lined with blue.

Dear Mike:

Here in Manchester it is even rainier than in Ithaca and the Jews here even the atheists all live together & go to school together (me included!). We wear uniforms recite prayers before lunch and get tons of homework. Everyone still calls me "The Yank" but it's OK I've got a few friends now. Hey Mike, if the difference between Judaism and Christianity is that Jews have to do something bad to be bad, not just think about it, then I think a woman can only rape a man if she's a Christian. You see? So wow, if you rape a man you turn into a Christian ha ha. But here's a tricky one: suppose I want to rape men but I know it's impossible? I fully intend to carry out the act, but the mechanics slip me up. So then I'm maybe a Buddhist, right?

In the dream Josh is between the walls. Inside them, walking from room to room as Mike teaches and sleeps and fucks through his day. Something happens, maybe Dead Josh talks, but he cannot remember it now. Sarah and Jessica and Renee are on the couch, practicing his new arrangement for L'chah Dodee, oh we greet you Sabbath Queen. They make each record in one day, that's the rule: Friday mornings, he writes the arrangement and sets up the equipment. He takes students until four, then the girls show up, rehearse, and then bang they record. However tanked up with pizza and giggles they start out, by the time their voices are cutting into the vinyl they are all voice, laying sound against sound faces pale. Sing with one voice. The bed overfilling with them, so many shaved legs and perfumed necks piling in. The more he knows their details their family sagas the specific curves of their hip bones their separate moans the more they are one voice. Sabbath queen we greet you as one. He is the Sabbath queen all in white, flesh glowing against the grey sheets. The Shehina is the female aspect of our god-term, the queen of the Sabbath who is the sabbath the rest the pause in god's week. Tanya only comes one Friday to make up a Wednesday lesson she'd canceled for a ballet recital and he is brisk. They are doing Hebrew grammar and like piano she never practices somehow thinks she can fake through it and he never yells but ends halfway through the hour. I've got a new really cool arrangement for L'cha Dodee we're gonna record tonight. Can I show you?

Rubbing tongues and cunts not fucking doesn't want fucking. Can't think of fucking them without imagining the little rips and slender tears they'd bleed home riding high on their new night licenses. The slow rubbery wetness of it hardening him watching their lips ready for the scream oh Christ fucking Christ yes sliding across not in them. Josh on top of some girl, Josh short and swimming in her, Mike walking in on them and Josh's eyes joking back to him, promising to save something for him. Like just because the song is about drugs the Eagles being totally about drugs doesn't make it not about pain at the same time chirps the blonde one you know some dance to remember, some dance to forget they harmonize their breath unfresh their voices gliding through him.

Everyone Moves in 1980

Tanya didn't realize it at the time, wrapped around her own family's shifting fortunes and a sudden urge to smush her toes in pink satin pointe shoes fourteen hours a day as she was, but after she left, the Ithaca Association of Jewish Studies was absorbed by the conservative Temple

Beth Israel with Rabbi Grossberg and his fully-catered Judaism by numbers. Mike left, Jessica left . . . she loses track of the rest, of where they left to. At the time she thinks Ithaca will leave her clean, wash off over the years as she rubs in other odors, larger cities. Seventeen, queen of the professionally alienated girls in black, insistently excitedly bored oh fucking bored by it all and the phone rings in the dorm room. It's your mother. Did Michael Silverstein ever do anything to you?

voluptuous anguish

This is precisely the whole problem: Attention has gradually shifted from the reevocation of Nazism as such, from the horror and the pain—even if muted by time and transformed into subdued grief and endless mediation— to voluptuous anguish and ravishing images, images one would like to see going on forever.

—Saul Friedlander, *Reflections of Nazism: An Essay on Kitsch and Death*

I performed for Mr. Kornblatt's camera. It didn't start that way. Like lots of girls, I loved to dance and sing and act. I loved the heat bathing my spinning form, adored the facelessness of the audience, craved the transformation of neighbors, family, and friends into a worshipping crowd. I performed in every student or community performance I could. From *Fiddler on the Roof* with the progressive Hebrew Studies Association to The Upstate Ballet's *Nutcracker Suite* at Christmas, there I was, twirling and smiling for the crowds, month after month.

Moira Kornblatt was another little girl. Like lots of girls, she loved to dance and sing and act. In *Nutcracker Suite*, she was the chubbiest mouse circling Clara and her Nutcracker Prince, double chin smiling out at the crowd. Her father came to our performances, anxious like all the other eager daddies to see his Moira twist and twirl, but it was me he shot.

He took an endless series of pictures of me, rolls of shiny Polaroids. There I am, shot after shot, my face sweaty and grinning, skin clinging to the sheer pink leotard. I was not a glamorous little girl, not one of those soft-skinned blonde sugar Hollywood confections. I sweated a lot, my pores opening like paper cuts, my coarse dark hair struggling to escape its tight ballerina bun.

Mr. Kornblatt would take a few perfunctory shots of Moira for every few hundred of me. He would slip a pack of them into my hand, each glossy photo carefully labeled on the back with my name, my age, the date of the performance, and some comments about my performance or the production. Tanya Irene Schwartz, age 12, 12/20/1978, performs the starring role of Clara in *The Nutcracker Suite*. She delights us all with her bouncy curls and graceful steps. Tanya Irene Schwartz, age 13, 9/13/1979, plays Tevya's youngest daughter in the Hebrew Studies Association's *Fiddler on the Roof*. Miss Schwartz stands out even in the poignant group numbers such as "Anatekva," her face as pure as her notes. One month after the production was over he would catch me after Hebrew school and press a manila envelope full of the photos into my hand. For your parents, he tells me with a quick kiss on the cheek.

He is only hands and arms for me. He touches my hands, his thick fingers squeezing mine tight, his fading number peering out from his shirtsleeves as he hands over the envelope and kiss, his breath surprisingly fresh for an old man. For him I am . . . Yona? I don't know when I decided that I was the image of his dead sister; perhaps between curtain calls for *Nutcracker Suite* and opening night of *Fiddler*.

I name her Yona. Yona appeared when Moira stopped dancing in our local productions and yet he still showed up at my concerts, armed with his cheap camera. I avoid the faded number overgrown with greying hair on his left arm. Yona was older than he, with my dark curls and bright eyes and heavy breasts. I overhear stories, whispers that Mr. Kornblatt had seen his brother be shot by the Nazis outside the gates of Auschwitz. No whispers about a sister, so I fill the space between those gates and the camera's shutter with Yona.

Yona with the sparkling black eyes and camera. Yona with a 1934 American model Leica or Brownie, photographing not people or places but spaces. Kitchen spaces. Beneath her lens, the inside of the kitchen cabinet became a smoky city landscape, the boxes of oatmeal and flour towering skyscrapers against a melancholy cupboard sky. Yona sequestered in the basement, elbow-deep in developing chemicals, swishing the paper under the fluid in time to the Strauss waltz on the radio.

"When the Nazis came," I imagine him telling his daughter Moira one Sunday morning before rehearsals for *Fiddler on the Roof*, "We thought Yona wouldn't be caught. We were eating our Sunday breakfast—herring in creme—when they broke down the door. She was already in the basement developing her pictures. But she was on their list." He pauses, slurping some coffee down with the bagels, his bathrobe sleeve riding up to reveal the tail end of his tattoo. "We lied, Mother protesting that Yona had gone to a cousin's in Frankfurt for the weekend, Father nodding furiously along with the story. And they seemed to buy it, more interested in pocketing Father's wristwatch collection than in accounting for the missing Fraulein. We were rounded up, sent that very night in the dirty train to Auschwitz . . . *Dayenu*. Enough." He is misty-eyed, unable to tell the rest of the story, how he saw his brother and mother shot, how he somehow wandered out of line for the gassing, the way a little blonde boy of five will trail off if not properly watched, how he wandered eight miles into town, sleeping in a haystack and pretending to be a toddler who couldn't speak in order to gain the affection of the Polish farmers.

"But Yona?" his flesh and blood daughter asks, gently, carefully.

"Ach, Yonichka . . . ."

Yona waltzing upstairs to join the family for breakfast. Yona at the stairwell, peering into the slashed furniture and empty room. Yona crying in the basement, developing her pictures, eating the props of oatmeal and flour. Hiding sleepless in the basement all night, singing to the Strauss waltzes on the radio. Making love to herself one last time, inhaling the chemicals from the developing fluid as she comes. Yona raped and beaten and killed by noon the next day. Did I read this story in one of those "Holocaust Artists" books, a glossy coffee-table number with pages of drawings and photos left in the camps after the gassings? Did Mr. Kornblatt?

•••

The lights have to be arranged just so to render the oatmeal box, cocoa container, and flower sack as a futuristic city skyline, silhouetted black against the grey wall. In the makeshift basement darkroom, the light is best just before sunrise, when the streetlamp that glares outside our house is dimmed. After these early morning sessions, I often fall asleep on the floor, granules of dirt pricking my skin while beside me my photos bathe in their murky developer fluids. Elaborate fantastic black-and-white cities invade my dreams, full of intricate buildings built of impossibly thin transparent materials. I dream of weightless cities unencumbered by gravity, full of slender women floating in silence through the walls.

Out of such a dream after such a night I awaken one morning. My throat is terribly sore, my head thumping with pain. Walking up to the kitchen with my throat thick and dry, I imagine tea with lemon working its way down my throat. From the landing I look in to the kitchen and stare at the broken chairs. Before the signs of struggle and pillage enter my eyes, I see the broken chairs. Cheap straight-backed chairs with orange cushions, bought or inherited before my birth so I have no idea from where they came.

...

I start performing for Yona. Extend my pointed toes and over-developed calves in arabesques toward her as I dance the *Nutcracker Suite* around a Christmas tree. Sing "Anatevka, Anatevka, intimate, obstinate, Anatevka" at the top of my range for her. Bow with extra fervor after each performance, hoping he will capture her in his cheap Instamatic, breasts peaking out over the chemical-filled basin as she develops yet another series of pantry interiors. As I smile at the faceless audience, Mr. Kornblatt appears behind the lens, capturing each glint of sweat across my bare thighs.

Tanya Irene Schwartz, age 14, 5/8/1980, appearing as the earthy Meg in Northern Junior High School's *Brigadoon*, adds extra zest to the role of the Scottish lass. Still the kiss and envelope, but I am dissatisfied now. I want a picture of Yona to put in a flowery ceramic picture frame I got from my Secret Santa at Northern. In a bookstore one day, shortly after *Brigadoon* had thankfully disappeared for good, I think I spot her: Yona in filmy pink, nipples showing through the leotard, staring unabashed at the camera. Yona staring pensively into the camera, impassive as the Nazis carelessly click on her beloved Leica before certain rape and death. But no, it's only a book of dance photography, full of little blonde ballerina girls peering big-eyed and winsome as the camera washes their budding nipples and leotards in a creamy pink light.

Back in the basement, the small space stuffed with all the provisions I could grab in a few minutes upstairs, I can't stop thinking of the chairs. I try to work as usual, finishing last night's photographs, making notes on changes in the position of the oatmeal box that will heighten the chiaroscuro effect for the next series I shoot. I focus too sharply, willing my brain to attend only to this darkroom, these photos. I am able not to think of where they are, what the Nazis do to five-year-old boys, whether they'll come back, but I find myself distracted by the family debris that has been stacked around the darkroom. Not my provisions, but the junk everyone has stashed down here, items not yet ready for the trash but no longer usable. I see an old pair of elegant black shoes of my mother's with one high heel missing. A discarded blue-and-white top of my brother's rests against it. I try to focus on the oatmeal box, but keep looking sideways to the heels and top. Finally I pick them up gingerly, as though they are made of glass, and place the broken shoe between the cocoa and the flour, and set the top beside the oatmeal box. I spend the afternoon staring at my assemblage, dropping off to sleep where I wander through my weightless cities with one broken high-heeled pump dangling from my foot.

•••

I awaken when the light is right. Aroused, restless, delaying full consciousness, I touch myself a bit too hard, rub to the point of sweet discomfort. I am relentless with myself. I cry out when I come, trying not to think of who might hear. And then I shoot: the last of my film wasted on a series of clearly un-citylike silhouettes, the shoe and top too round and curvilinear to be even the most alien, futuristic of buildings. Without realizing what I'm doing, I scoop out some oatmeal from the container, eat it raw and then discard the box into the corner. I realize I am waiting. And sometime during this afternoon which is now a blur, I heard the front door being smashed down and waited for their boots to pound down the stairs.

Mr. Kornblatt died recently. I didn't go to the funeral, but I had a dream in which he gave me a gorgeous framed photo of Yona after my dance recital. His breath was still remarkably sweet for an old man. He handed me the elegant frame instead of an envelope and kissed me directly on the lips. As I took the beautifully carved wood frame, I saw that instead of a picture of me, it contained his actual number, tattooed against his flesh, shining in the sugarplum pink of the photographer's lighting, the fading ink stretched tight to reach the corners of the frame.

spitbugs

I. In Season

Tanya never actually sees the spitbugs, so despite her after-school library research, she can never discover which phylum they might be. Jane is the spit bug expert, able to whisper their seasonal customs and intricate mating habits in Tanya's ear as they play hide and seek with the other kids in the tall grass behind their house.

●●

Tanya hides in the weeds, crouched down in a ball, waiting to be caught by the boy who is It for this round. Don't sweat. Jane's hands clasp her shoulders, pulling Tanya into an involuntary shrug. They're in season now, June being their favorite month. If you sweat, the spitbugs will sniff you out, their antennae wriggling toward you, picking up your coordinates from your salt. Let me hold you still so you don't sweat. Let me de-salt you.

II. Watch

Watch for the spitbugs, Jane calls between the cornflowers overrunning their family's vacant lot. Tanya follows the fake 200-watt gaslight that swallows the driveway out to where Jane is examining the weeds for signs of spit. Spitbugs are in season, she calls. Watch out! Jane pulls up the stalk of a long weed, the kind that look like green wheat. See their spray? She pulls thick spittle off the stalk, letting it cling to her forefinger, foamy and white as a home chemistry experiment.

They rustle through the weeds beyond the limits of the light. Jane stops, stoops down, Tanya immediately following suit. Watch out for spitbugs! And suddenly their mucus is covering Tanya, a swarm of spit swallowing her. Tongue, lips, those methodical teeth, all licking her with the determination of an exceptionally intelligent dog. Jane's thick lips drooling across Tanya's and spitbugs everywhere in season down her pants. The quiet of a lone diesel truck passing hums in the background. Green stalks glint with foam. Tanya's mouth awakens, abuzz, full of her all the way back to the tonsils. Spitbugs are everywhere. Tanya's tears mix with the saliva dripping its way down her face. I don't see any of your damn spitbugs, she sputters.

The tall grasses thicken with Jane's daylight sightings of their effervescing forms. This is the week. They are green, like Japanese beetles, but their eyes are something horrible. Tiny succubi nest under their eyes, closed tight by day, but at night they spit out streams of foamy mucus as far as fifteen feet. Jane's eyes opened so wide that Tanya sees the whole black pupil, a globe swimming in that glaring white as the spray of saliva strokes Tanya's cheeks again.

That summer they came out with instant iced tea, brown granules laced with white, vacuum packed in plastic jars tanned creamy like surf-song blondes. This is the week, Jane says with one eyebrow raised toward Tanya, when the spitbugs come and burrow their bluegreen legs deep into your neck. Jane reads the tea ingredients out loud: reconstituted lemon flavor, reconstituted flavor, guar gum, brown dye number four, and tannic acid. Tanyic, crows Jane, Tanyic Acid. Tanya eats it raw, lets little grains of tannic acid and artificial lemon stain dark outlines between her teeth. Their teeth: Jane's against hers, gulping down her tea-swathed tongue, bodies hidden together in a clump beneath the tall grasses in their untrimmed backyard where the spitbugs lie in wait.

III. Infestation

Tanya's bed is infested. Sticky evidence is left each morning of their travels across her bedding. At night they crawl into the bed, little green bodies wiggling like larvae inside her thin cotton underwear.

Between mouthfuls of iced tea mix, Jane checks for spitbugs the way they tell you to check for ticks and lice. After lunch, she surveys Tanya's body for hidden bugs that might record their conversations, forcing her square trimmed nails into the spongy places. Don't sweat. The bugs use sweat for electricity. OK Miss Tanyic Acid. You're clean.

At night Jane rolls over her as she sleeps, waiting to watch Tanya's eyes open wide like some curly haired baby doll designed to register surprise. Before Tanya jolts fully awake, Jane forces her lips open, tongue caressing the plaque forming over the tea stains on her teeth. The webby back of her throat hums the spit bug's insect virtues as Jane's teeth chatter against hers in the night air breezing into the bedroom from the backyard.

IV. Cure

The only way to cure yourself of spitbugs is to eat one at full glow. The spitbugs blink like an army of cigarette lighters against the clear June sky and Tanya prepares to swallow, but Jane insists they wait. It only works if you swallow it whole at full glow. Otherwise, their dismembered parts lie in your stomach, undigested for seven years like chewing gum. They squat beneath the thickest weeds that grow at the end of the driveway near the mailbox and wait. Tanya waits well. Loves waiting, feeling the sweat gather on the surface of her skin with each passing second. Jane palms one, stretching Tanya's tea-dirtied mouth open with her free hand.

Don't giggle, don't breathe, don't dare speak. And absolutely don't chew before you swallow. Just breathe it in as it glows—NOW!—like you're sipping a cool glass of tea. Tanya's incisors clamp down, piercing Jane's bug and finger together. Tanya twists out of her grasp, running up the driveway to the house as Jane wraps her finger in dandelion stalks. Dandelions are the antidote to spit bug bites, she calls after Tanya.

V. Hibernation

Spit bug season is over, Tanya announces at breakfast. Yes, Jane agrees, scooping out the bottom of the iced tea container with her finger. They're back in your mattress, burrowing between the fibers in hibernation.

It's silverfish season now, Jane notes as she licks under her nail. Silverfish have stingrays of mercury and they live in your shower, between the curtain and the liner. Only straight lemon juice immunizes you against them. Phylum: cordata! sings Tanya as Jane cuts a lemon in half with the sharpest steak knife. Silverfish are one of the only members of the phylum cordata, have two backbones, and can survive temperatures as cold as -40. They face each other, holding one perfect lemon-half each, and one, two, three together they dive their tongues into the bitter yellow.

sweet georgia

Georgia likes it when I fuck up. When she's angry she froths and foams, lips curled and twisty, limbs jerking intentionally out of the chair in quick spasms. People stop, thinking she's in pain, careful to avert their eyes from her twitching mass, pitying what they believe is an unwilled display of "disability." She likes grossing them out when she's mad. She works hard at it.

Yes, Georgia really likes it when I fuck up, or when things in general fuck up, are maddeningly delayed or chaotic or disorderly. Even when her bus is late and she has to wait at the curb with me, she laughs until she chokes,

●●

saying "you can't leave 'til it comes! you can't!" She laughs when change spills out of my purse, when I bang my shin on the side of her chair and curse, or when her bag slips off my exceptionally narrow shoulders. She tells me I'm too short. She doesn't like it when I take her swimming in the overchlorinated overheated Easter Seals pool whose water sticks to my sides like melted popsicles. She implies more than once that her father supports her leaden body with far greater ease than I ever can. She grabs my nipple through the thick water and laughs when I wince.

Tanya, do you believe in God? Georgia asks me one day when I've been there a while so she knows I can understand almost everything she garbles out. No. But there must be a God, everyone thinks so and if there isn't then it makes no sense. Do you have a boyfriend? Does he kiss you? She knows I won't tell her, knows I'm pretending not to understand her words as she spits them out near my ear like half-chewed sandwiches. She says she'd like me to come home with her so I could hit Constantine and Alexander, her younger brothers. She likes her name. Likes that it isn't Greek. Are you Greek? The Governor is Greek. Sweet Georgia Brown on my mind, I sing off–key as I force the milk container's straw up her mouth.

Georgia can't touch her pussy. When we go to the bathroom she laughs and tries to touch it. She watches my breasts. She's nine but already has some pubic hair. She's hairy in general. A big girl. An anatomical girl. When she paints, her clubbed fingers crash down on the paper, splattering blues and reds into each other. Baby blue is her favorite color. She knows I'm leaving for school in a week so she spits up on me even more than usual. I think of fucking her with a dildo; somehow I can't quite imagine my fingers toying with that hairy cunt between those twitching legs. I associate even the crudest mechanical aids with her body now, with the appliances that hook her soft brown flesh to the chair. Would she twitch if she came? Would I? Georgia, sweet Georgia on my mind, I whistle years later in front of a drugstore window filled with food processors.

plugged

Plug me up, she begs. He hates the words, silently wishes she could stick with the usual beat me fuck me grammar of such exchanges. Plug me up, Tanya pouts, and he does. Once plugged she ignores him, her eyes twitching under tight purplish lids as though in a fast-paced dream. It excited Benjamin the first time or two, that he could fuck the whole surface of her skin beat her scream right into her ears and she'd just lie there, plugged and twitching. He'd pretend she was dead, shout belligerently you're just a corpse I could skin you bury you cook you as he came in her hair.

●●

Actually, only her eyes twitch but he thinks of her whole body as twitching. Twitching, all of it, without exactly moving. Now it's the twitching within that plugged-up stillness that he craves, that makes him dream of her skin wrapping around his legs. Right now it's a skin thing, the thingness of her skin making him snap pencil after yellow number two pencil in half at his desk while he waits for her to call. Her skin is the border between secret dramas flickering beneath purple lids and his steady gaze over her not through her and the twitching is the evidence. Surveillance, I am the surveillance, he is repeating in his head this time when he comes on her chest.

In shopping malls she is inevitably seized by the desire to be plugged. Particularly on the elevators, the ones in those sleek silent malls which rove unprotected between floors, flying up and down with only the most minimal siding yes when she floats unmoored between floors clutching her brown paper shopping bags to her chest one hand steals below and above her thick leather belt to plug up anything she can. She carries tissues in her purse now for just that purpose, just in case.

Before, she didn't need much plugging. Before, Tanya would take a taxi from her office three nights a week sometimes four and head straight down to the Marquis or Zone or the Elevens and find a bench, any bench; it was important not to get too attached to particulars. In any corner on any bench she would pull out three thick leather belts and tie both calves then the waist then her wrists in square double knots to any bench and close her eyes tight and wait. She would not be splayed. She would not be plugged. She would not be naked. She would not speak. She would wait in her beige or grey or taupe work clothes, all three sections strapped down, arms stretched above her head. Bodies and hours would buzz past her. She was stopped; not frozen really, just stopped, still, like the four thickly painted walls through which it was all passing. And Tanya would wait and they would come alone and in groups up her skirt in her face in her hair across her nipples the accumulating dicks and arms and mouths weaving together holding her this skin a matrix for wet and motion.

Or so she remembers it now as she dials his number, and before it rings knows she will say it. Plug me up. Now the pluggings are absolutely necessary and occur with increasing frequency. Her mouth moves so fast these days as it forms the words snaking around each other eating themselves up with her anxiety? fury? focus? that he absorbs only their motion, the pushing out of those dry thin lips on *plug,* the tightening of her jaw on each *up.*

Plug me up plug me *up* words blurred against the whir of her mouth and
   winter starved trees rustle outside they
   could be your morning breath, voice slow, gritty, the
   mac truck passes *(driver pumped up on grainy sugar sweet*
      cocaine, throat too dry to match that country
      western radio as he pumps that gas pedal
      hard down this house a blur running
      tongue against parched lips leaning deeper

> *down into his custom-beaded seat*
> *remembering the taste of those wrinkled*
> *maps of veins behind your knees at dawn)*

quickly outside. (hurt me fuck me plug me now
Benjamin now)

There was that time: when blood vessels just beneath my
    fingertips would rise yeastily, puffing up into that
space
    behind your ear, that indentation
    Others lack;
(just plug me let nothing escape plug me up *now*—)
the heat there was tropical fermenting my heavy blood I
lick each fingertip in time to the passing traffic

> *(he's too*
> *damn high honey to feel the*
> *invisible bone white grains cutting into his*
> *nostril through myriad networks of*
> *crystal lattice*
> *piss elegant*
> *blood vessels oh sugar veins cartilage ignite*
> *oh sugar they expand in pink fury breaking skin*
> *as he pushes unevenly greyed lizard skin*
> *booted foot down hard on the pedal)*

    as the clock glows red 3:07, red 3:08 while my fingers
    write restless lines into my
    restless cheek
and he does.

And in cars. Yes in cars. Not on subways, so commuting to the office and back is generally safe but in cars she must be armed with the softest of tissues readied for the plugging, bunched up just so in her purse. I don't want to talk about it, she tells him. Just plug me fucking plug me up. And he does.

Back then, she would be aware only of the bench, its red plastic sticking against her skin, its surface cupping her in as endless flocks of bodies whirred and came, whirred and dripped over into through her. There was a friendliness to the bench. Its unchanging dimensions, the ugliness of its red paint, its scent of Clorox and sweat—all its trivial details repeating against her ass each night: however trussed or tied or fucked she might be the red would stay ugly red beneath her.

But now it's cars, Benjamin, she pants in a low whisper, in cars backing out of those grey-topped familiar driveways at a slow crawl or whirring along highways full of scenery that pass too quickly to reach that back of the eye where images root—in cars all cars I must plug me up fucking plug me up. Her throat stuffed to capacity now little shards of tissue trailing up and down the escalators plug me *up* and he does.

unter den linden

Kristellnacht wasn't advertised as a shootout. I walk through Kristellnacht's backyard, between bombed-out lots and thick ancient European walls riddled with bullet wounds, able to think only of being "fucked senseless" in quotes.

One forgets the bullets necessary for the shattering of such sturdy walls. Back in 1936, my grandfather lazily drinks his morning milchcafé, wondering as the walls shudder and he stirs in the sugar if perhaps it is thundering outside. As I walk through the old Jewish quarter I am invisibly fucked furiously by this Aboriginal Kori poet

●●

with his blond curls and grey eyes I met only hours ago. I finger the bullet holes as I walk and already I see us there, fucking silently like strangers don't fuck, hoping he'll know somehow to spread my lips as he thrusts in there no there. In the hundreds of accounts of Kristellnacht I've read, what is always emphasized is the shattering of glass that gives the night its name, rather than the pelleting of bullets gouged into the remaining walls. New knowledge exhausts me down to my toes. I insist that our party duck into the nearest coffee shop.

In the antique chandeliered café we sit in maroon velvet chairs, facing out on more buildings sprinkled with patterns of holes like a pointillist painting. Coffee fattened with fresh milk burns its familiar path down my throat as I slouch deeper into the velvet cushion. Forty no fifty years later, and still so ubiquitous, these first wounds of Kristellnacht. I am an artist, announces the mauve feminist haircut next to me. You see, I am an artist. A two-toned card is produced, expensively engraved on good Black Forest paper. I palm it, my Kori poet's perhaps uncircumcised cock between my thumb and forefinger, his beard scratching uneven patterns into my cheeks, a firm Euromattress holding it all in. I force my attention back to the bullet holes, but their fairy tale carvings of shattered glass and stormtroopers quickly fade as my leg accidentally brushes against his.

We must go the Volksbühne, the scruffy Kori poet says to me as we finish our coffee, and back in the 1973 orange shag family kitchen my father belts out *Volks are standing everywhere/We are the peat moss soldiers* in a mixture

of German and English. Interspersing the familiar tale of
my grandfather's escape from the evil Nazis as he sings
Marching to our graves / To the bogs, he carefully turns
the pancakes for Sunday breakfast in our orange shag
eat-in kitchen. *Not a soul comes out to greet us / Volks are
standing everywhere*, he sings, summoning a young mustachioed Grandpa calmly drinking his coffee as the glass
shatters around his unfurnished student room. *Marching
to our graves/To the bog.* He only thinks yes, I must leave,
when a fellow Jewish student rings his bell and swoops
him away to Switzerland on the train before the Nazis
can catch him. On the subway hurtling toward the Rosa
Luxemburg Platz that holds the Volksbühne Theatre
inside the new unified Germany, a smiling mustache calls
out in East Berlin German:

"Next stop is *Unter den Linden*, Under the Limetrees."
I tear myself from the tight-jeaned poet and fall out onto
the street with crowd.

Passengers tumble out onto the concrete plaza, walled
in by Bennetons and beer bars. Under den linden railways
sprout where limes fell. The station sign reads "Bergen
Belsen Auschwitz Treblinka" etcetera. Next to it another
sign reads, "All Jews were gathered at this exact spot for
deportation to various concentration camp sites across
Germany," proclaimed with the victor's certainty. This
spot? No, maybe this one? All Jews, every last one? Wait
under the sign for that next train, glide from U-Bahn to
S-Bahn, snake West to East, call out "next station under
the limes trees." Wait for me beneath the ghosts of trees
in that next station, Herr Fraulein sweetheart babydoll,

and I will be there ready to riddle your body with absent limes. Beneath my eyelids a faded black-and-white photo forms of that future grandfather, trotting along to anatomy class on a splendid sunny avenue lined by enormous trees groaning with ripe green fruit. I open my eyes to see the smiling, confused face of the beautiful poet, fumbling with his map to find the Volksbühne.

As we pile out of Unter den Linden Germans in various neon orange and blue and pink uniforms run in to fix things. There's something a bit elementary school about it: the caption in the child's primer: "Fireman Bob and Carpenter Roy work together to fix the broken drain in the train station," their bright identifying uniforms smiling out of the story. My Kori poet wants to shop the vintage clothes stores near Unter den Linden today, blow off the awful awkward conference droning on in the unheated basement of the Volksbühne. His right ear has a cut, a small triangle of removed flesh, in that webby part that is not the lobe. My tongue could carve into it, coat it solid. Could bite into it until his blood sugar level drops, my incisors not listening to reason, tearing up that careful triangle.

You see Doctor, I say to some imaginary capitalized doctor who always looks like Joyce Brothers in her sock-it-to-me *Laugh-In* incarnation, my fantasies always land me in the concentration camp. Clearly, I have survivor's guilt without having any real survivors to peg it on. Like Sylvia Plath: *you do not do, you do not do,* ach, du ... She raises her expensively waxed eyebrow. And the Jewish Question? she demands. I think I'm making it up, I confess as I stretch on that neon-orange couch: the grandfather, Kristellnacht, the Nazis, the bullet holes. It all seems so Hollywood, so improbable. I will the good Doctor away, back to the neverland America where Richard Nixon squeals "Sock it to *Me!*" for the pre-Watergate television in 1971. In the enormous department store overlooking Unter Den Linden Station, I look for something to take back. The Wall in a Bottle? Hammer and sickle pins sold two for a deutschmark? I like the five-inch black model East Berlin car and pocket it, the first thing I've officially stolen since junior high school. There are no swastikas for sale, no Jews to memento mori. "Remember Death!" the shrunken Jew in the glass bottle would declare in cheap pain embossed upon his prison uniform.

Have you gone on walkabout? he jokes as we hustle down the elevator, explaining that walkabout is when a Kori goes on dreamtime away from this clock and that narrative. Germany on walkabout. Kristellnacht sent my grandfather on walkabout, I tell him earnestly, leaving his world of anatomy class, beer halls, blonde frauleins for trains to Switzerland, Scotland, finally flying dreamily into the New World, Queens, Twin Willows, Miami. A new, bright yellow sign will be erected above the black and white ones which now dolefully mark where the Jews gathered for the trains: This is where Germany officially went on walkabout.

fabrications

i.

It's everywhere, all over uptown and the remains of downtown, printed on everything from silk to chenille, on everyone from the mayor's mistress to our hippie cat-sitter. On a do-rag arranged like a pirate's, cocked to one side. Printed big on a too-tight sweater, clearly acrylic. Spread across gym shorts, worn with nothing but sneakers. And don't forget those horrible pins, like old ladies wear when they want to jazz up their pants suits. A plague of flag.

ii.

You wear blue jeans that are too short and a rayon scarf that is too long. On Fifth Avenue, you do the impossible: you stand out. This is not the seventies.

You wear big earrings, glittery half-moons that pull your ear lobes to your shoulders. In Detroit, this is considered punk rock. You will not kiss and you will not swallow anything except diet soda and speedballs. This is not the eighties.

You wear both a nose ring and a ponytail. You play in a garage band that rhymes "dismay" and "day." You fuck without a condom. In a restaurant in L.A., you hum your dismay song as you fill up the ketchup jars and wait to be discovered. This is not the nineties.

iii.

I close my eyes and open them and you are standing over me, as if you've come upon an animal already stripped of meat and are wondering what to do with the skin. You kiss me on the cheek without looking at me, fulfilling the minimum requirements for a kiss.

"Where should we go for dinner?" You have killed the ponytail; there's a small dot that remembers the nose ring.

"Kono's?" I touch where a watch would go, feel your pulse. Is it fast or slow? I don't know how to read a pulse, but I like to pretend.

"Okay." You are tired. You are already in your jacket.

We talk animatedly on the way to dinner, but fall silent after we order. You are watching your weight, no steak. The street is jumping tonight. It's only Thursday, but everyone wants to find some spring in their evening. We both like these jittery city nights. We like our streets crowded and our pulses racing.

iv.

Nobody talks about it. It's like in those old WWII movies where someone walks down the street and everywhere are flags with enormous swastikas, uncommented upon by our heroine. A club girl with magenta hair and green platforms has made a skirt of it, barely nipping below her crotch. A fluffy bow, tricolored, in a little girl's long ponytail of gold. All done up in stars and stripes, red white and clashing blue. I prefer the old New York uniform, black on black, a pirate's plain flag.

v.

The hot water is coming out green and frothy. I lean into the tub to investigate. This is it, I tell myself as if I'm the heroine of my very own post-Cold War thriller: they've poisoned the water. I put a glove on, an old red mitten missing its mate. The water even smells green, herbal. Herbal? Unless the terrorists are using Herbal Essence shampoo as their weapon of choice, it's just a backed-up drain.

You like this story. You like my mistakes. You take off my glove and call me The Nose and swear my sense of smell is canine. You touch my back without thinking and if you did it again I'd be yours until the drain goes dry.

vi. Subject: Support our troops!

I'm on every liberal hit list in the country, and still I get this shit. I open the email; who can resist? The flag is placed at the center. It looks like a frosted cake, the colors thick and blurry, and for $4.99, it can be mine. *Fits right on your American car*, but I have no car, American or otherwise. I don't even drive; surely an act of treason. *Special deal: three for $12.99—Buy one for your home, one for your car, and one for your neighbor*. And one for the little boy who lives down the lane. *The money goes to the families of the victims of the World Trade Center*. They leave out the word 'bombing,' as if the building itself were the perpetrator.

vii.

I'd like to be dead, she says, but just for, oh, let's say a month. To test-drive death, take her for a spin around the block.

That sounds very ... American, you say. You are not alarmed. You and she have lots of conversations like this. You notice her jacket, a tight black wool number, boat-necked. It accentuates those thin bones on her neck. You smile at her neck.

Or do it scientifically: here is a month dead, here is a month alive. She is animated now, the bones are dancing. We could watch both, she says, split-screen. Compare and contrast.

Like a ghost?

No, like a person who is dead and not dead.

It sounds tiring, you think as you nod. And boring, like one of those early seventies college films with an extremely pregnant naked woman jumping up and down on a tatty bed, while "Strawberry Fields" played at 35 rpm in the background. There were three record players, two screens, and one joint. She was in blue on one screen, and I think red on the other. Watch too long and you get a purple headache.

You steal a sip of her coffee as she keeps talking, turn the strawberry film off, and imagine yourself lining her coat, cloth on one side, skin on the other, and you feel her neck stretching out of you.

viii.

Hey, remember that stupid war? How there were fucking flags everywhere, and we felt like we were trapped in a bad WWII movie? How everyone pretended George Bush was smart? Remember how right-wing and scary and just plain unsafe everything was? Remember being scared to open your Visa bill for a reason other than your balance? Remember seeing all your childhood fears on T.V.: planes exploding into buildings and people falling out of buildings and buildings crumbling until they're not buildings anymore?

ix.

After you pop your father's Viagra, examine his FY 1990-2000 tax returns, eat the vanilla almond Tofutti that's dying in the fridge, and wash it all down with expensive cognac, what else is there to do at 4 A.M. at your parents' house when you're 34?

You explore under their bed, of course.

Now what?

You sit naked at the kitchen table in your father's leather jacket. What time is it? They are in New Mexico California Montana. And you are here. What to do? Add shoes.

Your father is good for hiking shoes. All the spoils of an upscale sporting-goods store are yours. Running shoes, all-weather nylon pants, and those goddamn hiking shoes, cleated heavy as wooden clogs. Everything comes in small and large, no medium. Your father's house is fully equipped for a father/son hiking trip.

You put on his hiking shoes without socks. They don't go with the jacket. So take a tour. Pick up the pieces of dirt that fall off the shoes as you clomp across the varnished hard wood floors. If this house was yours, you'd ban varnish. If this house was yours, you'd lose the vaguely Mexican rugs, kill the brass hall lights, retile the bathroom floor in something less arts-and-crafty, and mix yourself a nice vodka-and-Prozac tonic. If this house was yours, you'd go to sleep.

x.

During the Stalinist era, the present vanished. Or, more precisely, it was erased. I'll explain: in 1937, they printed a new map of Moscow for the first time since 1927, but instead of putting what actually existed on the map, they put the future: everything that was supposed to be built in the city according to the coming 5-year plan. So to find your way to the grocery store to buy some carrots, you had to use the map of the past and the map of the future, and figure that the produce of the present lay somewhere in between.

xi.

You want the ambulances to come like racehorses on speed, swerving over the yellow line to get to you. First you have to . . . faint? Fall? No, something with a 'c'. Convulse? First you faint dead away, then you fall on the hard floor, then you convulse. A blanket is put around you, a blue polyester thing. Who chose it? Someone calls for the horses, *we have a situation here,* and still swaddled in blue, you drift from the scene, slipping away like a forgotten ghost.

xii.

We squint down Fifth Avenue. I notice there are others, also squinting. It's hard work, looking for what's not there. I hold your hand; I forget how warm flesh is, how solid you are. Let's buy scarves, you suggest, and yes, this is exactly right. Something warm, something to tie, something to help us find this disappearing world.

meredith

Dear Meredith:
Item One

Oh Meredith. I think you'd be happy to know I still wear the makeup.

Recall my nails tracing, retracing my pale face, framed in its curly tendrils. And you, keeping time to this fleshy metronome as your fingers move around your breasts, caught in the rapture of one of your endless self-exams. One of you will doubt me, you tell your left breast as you

●●

press in a circular motion counter-clockwise around the aureole. And one of you will betray me, you tell the right one, probing for suspicious lumps. Your fingers stand firm upon those pliant disciples, sternly investigating what might be growing beneath their visible surface to the beat of my scratching.

Afterwards, I'd apply creamy beige like a rag across the scratches and acne. Scars would form around the pancake, crusting up with Maybelline and the rest. Even when scrubbed clean, the scars would cling to those thick off-white molecules. You must recall the constellations. Mary Jane, Anne Marie, Marika . . . when the scars stopped healing you connected the dots, tracing out constellations between the blotches in the shape of girls named Mary.

What else to report? The charge you always levied against my hair—that its thick black curls were obscenely, explicitly pubic, thus making my mouth, well, the obvious thing—has finally proved true. As I grey, the hairs turn thicker, even curlier, bunching around my still-unwrinkled face in the familiar triangle. I look in the mirror and think of you stroking my hair, my hands, and oh, my Meredith. Do you still think of the dirty joke my hair became? Or are such details erased now, their kinks (forgive the sorry joke; it's yours, after all) long straightened?

Another new development: the eyelash tugging has traveled up. You'll recall the scene vividly. Staring into the mirror, thick fingers snug around lash after elusive lash, eyes glazed wide open. Tug tug, pull: stubborn, like pulling out a teenage boy's beard a hair at a time. Repeat until lashless. Red circles like eyeliner, circling and then replacing the fringe. Anxious for the first slender fresh ones to sprout only to begin the pulling again.

And Meredith, my sweet Meredith, you there in the door, watching without comment. Touching the sore pores at night. Outlining my small, hairless body with your fingertips. Well, it's traveled up at last, straight up to the hairline. Tugging out acres of eyebrows and stray facial hairs along the way.

Forgive me.

I am unlovely tonight.

Digestion begins on the tongue. Those unpronounceable enzymes breaking you down as your tongue wrestled mine, tasting that sharp mintiness left over from the Colgate with the French label you'd buy at the wholesale store. Combat la carie. Dentifrice au fluorure. Probably from Haiti, you would say, filling your mouth with white Francophone foam. Made in Queens, shipped to Haiti, lay on the shelf a year in Port-au-Prince, expensive and unsold in its red-and-white wrapper. And now back to Brooklyn at half the price. My mouth is well-traveled, you tell me as you rinse in my sink. You have a distinct aftertaste. Vive la France. Mint, and something else: metallic. Like the silver on an old dime. I won't embarrass you with tales of my tongue licking spare change late into the night trying to recover that flavor.

Lest you think this is simply another of my rambling letters of which you will read choice portions to the latest blank blonde propped up on your bed, let me assure you this is actually a business letter.

Item Two

I want whatever it was you promised me.

Whatever glues the make-up on. Whatever keeps the mint fresh on your tongue. Your mouth, my hand. When you left it washed right off, leaving no sweet scent wafting in the corners of my apartment, no film on my skin. My Meredith. I remember you here, minty and napping, promising me that thick syrupy substanceless thing that binds. I thought you had infected me with it, that it was spreading your promises through—what do they call it? Parasitic transcription? Not wiping your hands from the washroom? Phantom limbs? Influenza B? Your fingers interlaced in mine. Indistinguishable. Cheek to cheek, vein to gristle. One foreign cell absorbed by another, repeating its secret code under my fingernails. You the fur-clad Russian agent, I a steely-eyed Bond. My hands, your mouth. I thought you were replicating night and day in my cells, minty fresh discounted from Haiti, day and night you were the one.

Item Three

And you were.

Item Four

And so you left me here, contaminated. Chemicals pissing down my brain. Little grains of sour white and yellow god-knows-what dripping together so I don't know if it's the illness or the pill piss or your French mint mouth giving me such a godawful headache. I try to discern the kick of each, the moment the red sugar-coated one changes my sinuses or mood, that instant the plain rough white ones start to pep me up . . . or were they supposed to slow me down? I'm up and edgy, that's for sure. Playing with my room, flipping books open and shut, changing earrings and changing them back, touching all the surfaces as if checking for dust. I suddenly want to puke, then piss, then just hold still and feel the chemicals piss their way down my brain. It's my room for sure, my black jeans sprawled over a chair, my mess of lipstick and antique wrist watches on the dresser with my pills, but there's something missing here. Or extra.

Everything is numb. I lie naked, flesh greenish, sprawled on my stomach. The pill piss increases its stream, making my head throb. I notice that I can't touch my head, or rather I can "touch" my "head," but it is like one phantom limb touching another. It is as if my whole body has been severed, and I am just feeling its echo. I must pee, must pee, dins a voice in my absent head. I squeeze those intricate muscles like a fist around a sponge, waiting for the watery relief to stream out. But it's not me; it's you. Your body made into my flesh.

Oh Meredith. You have replaced me. But this is strictly business.

Item Five

As I said, I want what you promised me. Make me your identical twin. Wed our DNA at conception. My hands, your hands. Even though we were the same height, your caresses always emphasized my shortness. My own Rita Hayworth, cut short at the knees, you croon as you caress my hair. I try not to breathe. To fix us here beneath your thick palms. But you have evacuated. You with your teeth in such delicate ruins, lying half-buried in your gums. You promised everything in its place and a place for everything. My tongue so comfortable against your unfilled cavities. My tongue quiet.

I walk by the Spanish-Portuguese Jewish Cemetery off Seventh Avenue. Barely a dozen graves still stand, faces erased, boxed in by fences from the parking lot to the left and the expensive condos to the right. 1821-1857, reads the sign above the fenced-in remainders: a short window of time for the dead to accumulate. Only a dozen graves left over so many Spanish-Portuguese Jewish bones, I tell you, worried. Marika, Marilyn, Mary-Claire, I rename the smooth white stones. They moved them to the suburbs, you promise, fingertips pressing out the wrinkles in my forehead. Reinterred their aching Ladino bones in comfortable, frequently watered and trimmed plots just an exit off the Sunrise Highway. But I know better now.

I learned it slowly, from the Quebeçois toothpaste, one brush at a time. French and English would seem to be perfectly balanced, symmetrically splashed in red and white across the label: Regular/Populaire. Fights Plaque with brushing/Combat la plaque lors du brossage. But the disfiguring asymmetries coalesce with regular usage. Questions? 1-800-268-6757, says the fine print, with no French translation.

Something escapes automatic translation. And has left me without you. Yet here I stand in your used hiking boots, brushing my yellowing teeth full of your cavities. You beat me at me own game, like the rhythmic impersonal slaps of a professional dominatrix. You win me away from you with each silver filling implanted where your tongue should be.

Piss and moan, you say as you read this. And I do. For I keep my promises with every trip to the lavatory, every brush with the Colgate. My hair curls thicker than ever, waiting for your dirty jokes. I want it back, Meredith. Your promise. My hands, your mouth. And I mean business.

thirteen fugues

i.

The dirtied bluish linens. The inherited garnet jewelry. The books and notes I can't possibly have written. The red cough syrup without a label. There is too much red here. I can't remember myself, can't imagine choosing these objects, their little histories, my preferences. This is my bathroom, I tell the towel rack. This is not amnesia. I am only experiencing minor delays, like a single-engine

●⓪●

jet grounded due to inclement weather. Driving in aimless circles, a low-hanging fog obstructing transmission between synapses, I open and shut these cupboards, my cupboards. But what is my name?

ii.

The Reverend Ansel Bourne* of Green, R.I., was brought up to the trade of carpenter; but, in consequence of a sudden temporary loss of sight and hearing under very peculiar circumstances, he became converted from Atheism to Christianity just before his thirtieth year, and has since that time lived the life of an itinerant preacher. He has been subject to headaches and temporary fits of depression of spirits during most of his life, and has had a few fits of unconsciousness lasting an hour or less. Otherwise his health is good, and his muscular strength and endurance excellent. He is of a firm and self-reliant character, and his charter for uprightness is such that no person who knows him will for a moment admit the possibility of his case not being perfectly genuine. His sudden assumption of the character, name, and trade of one "A.J. Brown" was an unprecedented act for which his prior disposition bears no precedent.

---

* Some of Bourne's language is culled from a case history by William James. See James' *Psychology* (New York: Henry Holt, 1893).

iii.

It is an argument like any other argument. Our ears shut tight to one another, impenetrable as newborn cat's eyes.

You're not listening, I say.

I can't hear this now, you say back.

Something dull and vague replaces the complicated twists of argument. The switch flips, the bottom falls out, the dynamite sizzles. I am seized by I can't stay here go must leave. Choking on the walls, suffocating beneath those thick layers of white paint slathered on for each new tenant who occupies this room. Falling forward can't stay have to leave must get on the bus.

Tanya, you sigh, your terrible calm only igniting it further.

I find myself on the street, face dripping tears, feet racing toward nothing at all. Liner notes to Bach's *The Art of Fugue* dart in and out of my head, keeping time to the slap of my soles on the pavement. In a fugue, a musical theme or phrase is transposed a key, inverted, or repeated with slight alterations. The volume turns up in my head, must leave must leave pulsing through my veins, each syllable hammering out a syncopated rhythm against the slap of my running feet. The original melody elaborated, reduced, returned; yet still distinct, recognizably related to the original. Panic ices through me: I have left I am falling forward to no certain destination must leave must leave can't remember my name. Different sub-classifications of fugues drum in my head: tonal, real, must leave must leave.

In a fugue I walk toward the bus station, any station, any bus driving against the noise repeating in my skull. I hate buses, the smell of them, the war vets with stale tales and sick aunts, shoulders cramping against the high back of the seat. Must leave must leave burns through me, propelling me forward as the street grows blurry through my tears.

But fugues split hairs. There are real fugues and tonal fugues and endless arguments regarding which is which. The real fugues transpose invert repeat the same melodic structure; the tonal ones change the original melody in the process. Some argue tonal fugues are the true if not real fugues, since the complex transformation of melody through fugal response is precisely the point of the fugue in the first place. My mind is calming, the beat of must leave slowing as I seize on the problem of defining fugues. Not to mention fugue states, that favorite malady of Victorian America, traveling under a new identity in a trance-like state to another geographical as well as psychic state. From Providence to Pennsylvania, from upstanding citizen to wild-eyed preacher, fugues change the original, pulse their maddening repetitions through the foreheads of proper New England gentlemen.

My feet stop at the West Side Highway. The Hudson is brackish today, a thick grey carpet connecting the posh quiet of suburban living-rooms to the off-key hum of urban apartments stacked up like old newspapers. Hills jut up across the water, the bedrooms of Washington Irving, Sleepy Hollow, Rip Van Winkle nestled in their greenery. I am not at the bus station. Your arms do not surround me and I cannot find my name.

iv.

On January 17, 1887, Mr. Bourne drew 551 dollars from a bank in Providence with which to pay for a certain lot of land in Greene, paid certain bills, and got into a Pawtucket horse-car. This is the last incident which he remembers. He did not return home that day, and nothing was heard of him for two months. He was published in the papers as missing, and foul play being suspected, the police sought in vain his whereabouts. On the morning of March 14th, however, at Norristown, Pennsylvania, a man calling himself A.J. Brown, who had rented a small shop six weeks previously, stocked it with stationery, confectionery, fruit and small articles, and carried on his quiet trade without seeming to anyone unnatural or eccentric, woke up in a fright and called in the people of the house to tell him where he was. He said that his name was Ansel Bourne, that he was entirely ignorant of Norristown, that he knew nothing of shop-keeping, and that the last thing he remembered—it seemed only yesterday— was drawing the money from the bank in Providence.

He would not believe two months had elapsed. The people of the house thought him insane; and so, at first, did Dr. Louis H. Read, whom they called in to see him. But on telegraphing to Providence, confirmatory messages came that indeed this man was Mr. Bourne, and presently his nephew, Mr. Andrew Harris, arrived upon the scene, made everything straight, and took him home. He was very weak, having lost twenty pounds of flesh during his escapade, and had such a horror of the idea of the confectionery store that he refused to set in it again.

v.

From the moment Jane Schwartz first heard the word, she was in love. *Epilepsy*. It is not the -ectic fits she adores, but the simple state of it. Swooning into epilepsy, hyperventilating until the floor moves up to her forehead and I'm floating, I'm flying! she cries as she leaps down a full flight of orange shag-rugged stairs into the refinished basement. Her epilepsy always involves these peculiar travels down the stairs, out of bed, off the sidewalk, even out the front door one time. Swift trips, yet dangerous, accompanied by multiple bruises and concussions. They try pink pills, no-sugar diets, even meditation. Still the epilepsy seizes her, dancing through her blood stream, causing fits and fainting and flying to erupt unprovoked as it pulses through her pony-tailed forehead. After six months of it, Dr. Anderson squints down at her through his thick black-framed glasses and utters the one word her parents have been aching for. *Specialist*. The epilepsy needs a specialist.

Will she pass the test? Will those infinitesimal samples of saliva DNA ear wax scraped from her pores provide the evidence, the raw data proving her epilepsy true? Will they uncover a slender white-boned growth under the left ventricle of her brain, a specimen as lovely as those full-color portraits of malignant tumors hanging on the walls of Dr. Anderson's office? As they speed on the highway north to Syracuse, Jane misses the menthol scent of Dr. Anderson's waiting room, the probing fingers with their too-long nails, that slight intake of breath before he gives the diagnosis.

It was a cold seduction. The epilepsy would caress her at will, driving Jane out of bed, forcing her hand to grab empty band-aid boxes shove them down the downstairs toilet and flush, flush until she hears the plumbing argue with the metal lids. Abandoning her on the stairs, leaving her stomach to burn under her thin plaid pajamas while the bathroom floods, the seizures and fits would suddenly evaporate. Unrepentant epilepsy. Don Juan of diseases.

Or was it only unrequited love? Perhaps the epilepsy ignores her calls, allowing her seizures to fall on deaf ears? Epilepsy rides into the sunset, a classic country-western heartbreaker. I worried. Sitting diagonally across from Jane, nails just beginning to form over my soft toes, I shift against the red-hued walls, anxious and unable to sleep beneath my shut lids. Moored in my warm bath inside my dark sac inside the small brown Datsun rushing over the speed limit toward the Syracuse neurology specialist, I picked at my new toenails and wondered why the epilepsy didn't want to call her. Maybe it just didn't know her name. But what is my name?

vi.

The first two weeks of the period remained unaccounted for, as he had no memory, after he had once resumed his normal personality, of any part of the time, and no one who knew him seems to have seen him after he left home. The remarkable part of the change is, of course, the peculiar occupation which the so-called Brown indulged in.

Mr. Bourne had never in his life had the slightest con-
tact with trade. 'Brown' was described by the neighbors
as taciturn, orderly in his habits, and in no way queer. He
went to Philadelphia several times; replenished his stock;
went regularly to church; and once at a prayer-meeting
made what was considered by the hearers a good address,
in the course of which he related an incident which he had
witnessed in his natural state of Bourne.

vii.

Janie Walkerson, or Wilkerson, or maybe Patterson.
Named like Jane Schwartz for Jane Russell, for whom all
the Janes' mothers shared a passion. I was in labor and I
was set to name you Ophelia—something real different,
Jane's mother tells her. But the lady sharing my room in
the hospital was naming hers Jane and when my water
broke, Jane Russell was on the T.V., and I thought you'd
have her dark hair and lovely lips and you do.

Jane Schwartz resisted Janie, remained resolutely Jane
from the start, grateful so few nicknames could be produced from such a short name. Janie Walkerson, Willison,
Peterson didn't mind 'Janie,' so Jane never thought of her
as a Jane. Janie's mother had Angie Dickinson white-
blonde hair with a middle part and a different big white
American car each week, everything opening and closing with the push of a button. She was a driving mom,
addicted to the parade of fat white cars she borrowed from
the show room, bargaining over the kitchen phone for FM

radio, plush carpeting, and a full tank from the latest used car-dealer husband who Jane never met.

Rugs crawled over every surface of the Patterson, Peterson, Wallerson house. Janie's thick pink shag rug trapped Barbie frying pans and hair pins in its synthetic arms but the Janes never played house with Barbie; she was used only for amputations and deliveries. Riding on top, Janie cries okay we have a boy coming out pulling her hands out of her cotton underwear as a chorus of mid-wife Barbies look on. Janie always the doctor, Jane beneath her thinking of Janie's mother driving a big white car. G.I. Joe, stripped of his camouflage and Uzi, emerges feet first, square jawed and fully bearded.

I don't want a boy, Jane tells Janie; put him back in. And up he travels: plastic head first, the synthetic fibers of his beard scratching inside her. Janie pushes, but he's stuck, his shoulders too broad, too muscle-bound to fit. He's a mutant from Jupiter invading by air! Send him back to his spaceship! Jane looks down for a quick second, catching a glance of Joe's black-booted feet swinging out of her, feeling the scratchy pink carpet press into her back.

Those long pinked months before I was born I would test toe nail, thumb nail against the walls like some old movie scientist locked up in a musky laboratory inside a starless night. Jane thought of me like the deaf, dumb to the sneers lacing her answers, or like the blind, shut eyes peering out of my amniotic sac at her, not noticing whether or not it was a new jumper Jane put on today. Chipping away inside, testing and carving my way about while Jane is deflowered several houses away by Barbie and G.I. Joe in the thick jungle pink of Janie's floor, I absorb every shudder traveling up her spinal cord. Each scratch of the carpet tickles my still-forming central nervous system, radiating a quiver from my neck to my nailless toes.

viii.

This was all that was known of the case up to June 1890 when I induced Mr. Bourne to submit to hypnotism, so as to see whether, in the hypnotic trance, his 'Brown' memory would not come back. It did so with surprising readiness; so much so indeed that it proved quite impossible to make him whilst in the hypnosis remember any of the facts of his normal life. He had heard of Ansel Bourne, but "didn't know as he had ever met the man." When confronted with Mrs. Bourne, he said that he had "never seen the woman before." On the other hand, he told of his peregrinations during the lost fortnight, and gave all sorts of details about the Norristown episode. The whole thing was prosaic enough; and the Brown personality seems to be nothing but a rather shrunken, dejected, and amnesiac extract of Mr. Bourne himself.

ix.

It was a boat house, not a house boat. An unwrecked ship surrounded by green lawn, with a fleet of white American sedans trailing up the driveway like a school of overfed fish

❶❶❶

to the anchor-shaped front door. Each bedroom had two porthole windows, and Janie's mom's room had a golden bathroom. The toilet, not just the seat but the toilet itself, was a particularly realistic-looking shade of gold, thick and metallic. The seat was made of a squishy substance that sighed when she sat. Jane avoided that bathroom; she could never shake the feeling as she eased herself down to the seat that she was pissing on an expensive couch. Janie's mother liked Jane to sleep over on Friday nights. Frosting her lids with blue, pasting on lashes one at a time, bleaching the roots of her Angie Dickinson, Janie's mom would leave before supper, mumbling instructions for the T.V. dinners and bedtime protocol as she sailed the white Buick, Chevy, or Ford out of the driveway. After a midnight movie and a round of Barbie and Joe, the girls would collapse in the den, sleeping on the beige modular couches.

It was the mornings that Jane loved on these overnights, early mornings in the kitchen making breakfast. The kitchen was a pastel heaven of children's cereal of every sugar-coated flavor, color television that always seemed to have the *Flintstones* opening sequence playing, and three different kinds of chocolate milk mix. By seven A.M. Janie Patterson or Walkerson, her hair frizzing out of a dirty blonde pony tail, would shake Jane awake, eager to give the grand kitchen tour. She opens each cupboard, displaying a virtual grocery shelf of sugar cereals, every flavor you'd please; seven picnics' worth of chips and onion dip; a rainbow of soda pop, from the predictable brown colas to hot fuchsia strawberry. A sugar-coated heaven accompanied by the high-pitched squeals of wall-to-wall

❶❶❶

Saturday morning comics. Janie's brother, Jamie, Jason, Johnny, ignored all night, would suddenly materialize in front of the cereal boxes, lodged on a shelf just out of his reach. Let's play invalid, Janie says. Johnny, you're too sick to eat so Jane has to eat your food for you.

Janie immobilizes Johnny, Jimmy, Jake in a neck lock in under thirty seconds; tries to force Jane to spit down his throat without losing her grip on her squealing brother. I . . . gotta go to the bathroom, Jane apologizes as she slithers away, grateful for once for the squish of the gold seat. Strains of Mighty Mouse here to save the Saturday morning T.V. echo through the house as Janie chews pastel cereals down his throat. Jane sits on the gold toilet even though she doesn't have to go, eyes clenched shut, waiting for the epilepsy to wrap around her.

I worried for Jane. Epilepsy was, after all, so terribly fickle. I thought Jane might dissolve down to her pink pajamas and silver baby tooth fillings as her ass slouched against the gold. What if she were trapped there, huddled on the gold toilet which didn't even flush properly, convulsing alone in the boat house moored on the trim green lawn? Or worse, what if the epilepsy refused her calls? From inside my red sac several houses away, I'd kick with anxiety as I heard Janie call for her, offering to make her a special mixture of all the cereals together.

x.

During the trance he looks old, the corners of his mouth
are drawn down, his voice is slow and weak, and he sits
covering his eyes and trying vainly to remember what lay
before and after the two months of the Brown experience.
"I'm all hedged in," he says: "I can't get out at either end.
I don't know what set me down in that Pawtucket horse-
car, and I don't know how I ever left that store, or what
became of it." His eyes are practically normal, and all his
sensibilities about the same in hypnosis as in waking. I
had hoped by suggestion to run the two personalities into
one, and thereby make the memories continuous, but no
artifice would avail to accomplish this, and Mr. Bourne's
skull today still covers two distinct personal selves.

xi.

For weeks after the visit to the specialist, Jane intercepts
the mail every afternoon when she comes home from
school, scanning each bill for a Syracuse return address,
sniffing each envelope for the telltale scent of hospital food.
She turns down requests from first Janie, then Janie's
mother, for her attendance at Friday overnights, fearful
that she will miss the Saturday morning delivery. Careful
to draw no attention to her surveillance, she replaces the
unopened mail in its metal box at the end of the driveway after each investigation. Before she investigates, she
puts on a mailman outfit: her father's old grey fishing cap,

her grandmother's tan suede jacket with crocheted buttons and wide lapels, an old pair of black stiletto heels her mother has donated to the dress-up box. Nothing too redolent of "spy."

Three weeks and four days after the visit, it arrives. A slim manila envelope smelling of rubbing alcohol, it arrives on a Tuesday with the hospital's return address and a Syracuse postmark. She opens it on the kitchen table. Forty-three minutes before her mother will be home from work, according to her digital wristwatch.

The first page is only a bill. She reads each word slowly. The second page is a series of numbers and multisyllabic words, titled *Test Results*. The third page is the charm: *Diagnosis*. EKG reveals *no* signs of epileptic brain activity. Hypothalamus appears to be functioning normally. Slight enlargement of right ventricle of the upper cerebellum. The epilepsy is rising in her throat, threatening nausea, blackouts, tears. Cheeks reddening into cherry circles, throat gripping tight, she runs to the remodeled basement bathroom. Maybelline Snow Frost White floods her nose with a sweet burn of isopropyl alcohol and perfume. Painting it, brushing that *no*, coating *no* with a soft snow frost white painting three layers over no until *Diagnosis:* EKG reveals signs of epileptic brain activity.

Epilepsy slips away as Snow Frost White hardens. The red carpet burns on Jane's butt. She stares at her tongue in the mirror. There is too much red here. She leaves the last of the epilepsy in the bathroom. Donning the unspy hat and coat for a final visit to the mail box, she folds the papers back along their original creases, closes the envelope, and

❶❶❹

proceeds to place it carefully back in the mailbox. She is hungry for cereal, for the Lucky Charms Coco Puffs Barbies G.I. Joes choked undigested down Janie's brother's throat.

xii.

The case (whether it contains an epileptic element or not) would apparently be classed as one of spontaneous hypnotic trance, persisting for two months. The peculiarity of it is that nothing else like it ever occurred in the man's life, and that no eccentricity of character came out of it.

xiii.

The grey waves of the Hudson are turning black. The pounding has vanished. I did not feel it receding; only once it is gone do I notice that the bus no longer beckons.

I imagine your expression at this moment. I see you washing the dishes in the kitchen, oversoaping each fork as you are liable to do in a catastrophe. Gestures play across your face as you silently recall the fight, mouth occasionally twitching, eyes tearing over.

My feet run towards home. *Tanya Tanya Tanya.* The trochaic meter of my name provides a hummable soundtrack to my steps, right foot stamping out the stress of the first syllable. The pavement is jeweled with broken glass, embedded in the asphalt like carelessly mounted diamonds. Good night, I whisper. Good night.

Breinigsville, PA USA
08 April 2011
259512BV00001B/1/P